SIREN
Publishing

Ménage Everlasting

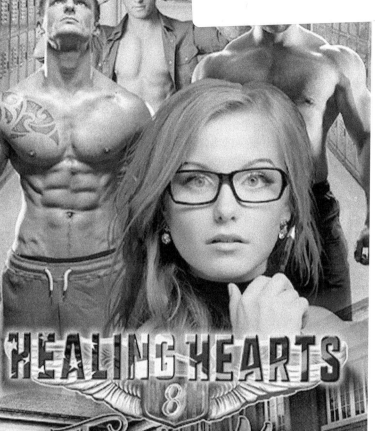

HEALING HEARTS
8
Teach Me What Love Is

DIXIE LYNN DWYER

Healing Hearts 8: Teach Me What Love Is

Faith doesn't know what real love is, and neither do the three older men she falls for. They may be older and more experienced, but none of them are prepared for love or the danger attached to it. Faith was beaten by the one man she thought she loved. She's a shy school teacher and Rocky, Paulie, and Hendrick are the epitome of intimidation. They are older, experienced, and cocky. They say opposites attract, but it seems all four of them need to learn a lot about love, and perhaps desire gives them the open door they need to learn.

Faith has loved and been betrayed. Rocky, Hendrick, and Paulie lost a brother to an addiction and his lost opportunity at falling in love and starting a family. When they meet Faith they think they can run the show despite how different it feels to be with her. Soon the teachers become the taught, and they all heal from their pasts and learn to love just in time to have it all taken away by a man from her past. Can their love help them to survive this? It's all on the line but even timid, shy Faith has learned a thing or two from her soldier, SWAT boyfriends, and she's willing to die to protect them.

Genres: Contemporary, Ménage a Trois/Quatre, Military, Romantic Suspense
Length: 46,038

Healing Hearts 8:
Teach Me What Love Is

Dixie Lynn Dwyer

Siren Publishing, Inc.
www.SirenPublishing.com

A SIREN PUBLISHING BOOK

Healing Hearts 8: Teach Me What Love Is
Copyright © 2018 by Dixie Lynn Dwyer
ISBN: 978-1-64243-539-9
First Publication: October 2018
Cover design by Les Byerley
All art and logo copyright © 2018 by Siren Publishing, Inc.

Siren Publishing, Inc.
www.SirenPublishing.com

DEDICATION

Dear readers,

Thank you for purchasing this legal copy of *Teach Me What Love Is*.

Faith has a broken heart. She has lost what little confidence she had and fears that she can't read people, especially men, and determine if they want to use her or actually care. Her shyness and sweet demeanor seem to be a target for aggressive men.

After being hurt by an ex-boyfriend, she surely doesn't want to experience such pain ever again. So she focuses on being a teacher, on the children in her class whom she adores, and prefers being alone more often than not. It's when her friends harass her about hanging out, and it becomes too much to ignore, that she gives in and goes out with them.

When she feels an attraction like nothing she has ever felt before to three brothers, she is hesitant to give into the sensations. Rocky, Hendrick, and Paulie are older, more experienced, and willing to learn more about this sexy little school teacher, with her designer eyeglasses, her baby blue eyes, and a shyness, yet sophistication that pulls on their protective strings. One kiss, and a few doses of jealousy, and they're hooked. Can they convince her to take a chance with them?

Faith wants to know what true love is, and whether or not it really exists. Her fears are authentic, and her fight to protect a broken heart make it difficult for these three men to show her that love is real.

May you enjoy Faith's journey.

Happy reading.

HUGS!

Dixie

ABOUT THE AUTHOR

For all titles by Dixie Lynn Dwyer, please visit
www.bookstrand.com/dixie-lynn-dwyer

Healing Hearts 8: Teach Me What Love Is

DIXIE LYNN DWYER
Copyright © 2018

Prologue

Andrew Price sat in his truck across from the elementary school. Mercy was a quiet beach town. A place where families loved to raise their children. Where they felt safe and secure with the local police patrolling and basically very low crime rates. That unrealistic perspective made these people sitting targets. If he had his sniper rifle, he could knock them off one after the next and no one would know where it came from. He felt uneasy just thinking that. His focus was on his little beauty. The sweet, sensual blonde, as she watched the little kids playing and received hugs on her legs against the long floral skirt she wore today. His woman, or at least she used to be.

Faith was everything to him. She kept him sane, calmed him, but the demons were too powerful. The stresses of life and what he wanted, what he deserved cost him everything. Including almost his sanity. That was why he needed her, or at minimum to see her, to watch her, to know she was there and that when the time came he could have her once again. He needed to be patient though. He was working too many things right now. Today was a risk, coming here, seeking her out. He drove the three hours but it was worth it. A whole year passed and his woman looked even more beautiful.

She didn't know how gorgeous she was, how appealing. So shy and innocent, a virgin. His virgin he never had the opportunity to claim because he screwed up. In his job, in his relationship with her, and securing his hold on her heart and on her soul. He would work on that now and from a distance. She would get his first gift soon enough. He would get her to forgive him, to accept his apology and then accept him in her life again. It would all come back together. He would fix it all.

She would be with him now if he hadn't struck her, beat her, took his rage and anger on his boss out on her. He was too caught up in the people he owed money to, and what needed to be done to finish off his deal with Greg. He wasn't going to settle for a shake of the hand and a "see ya," "good luck next time," or some other load of bullshit. He was more than capable of handling the jobs. That corporate asshole Leonard Strayffer gave orders, declined Andrew for the higher paying job because he was anti military, plain and simple. The fucking hippie bastard and his fellow business buddies were all haters.

Well, he would show them. Andrew was making a plan, and thanks to his best friend Greg, he would be able to hit Leonard and his buddies where it hurt most, the wallet, but also in their personal lives. In fact, Leonard's wife should be getting the threatening letter and dead animal right about now. See how he handled that. Plus the pictures of Leonard going into the hotel room when he was supposed to be at work should piss his wife off big time. That should leave the cops with some interesting investigation, and one leading to a mistress. Greg's idea, but Andrew's was much more violent and ended with torturing Leonard and listening to him beg for his life and offer Andrew everything he wanted and deserved.

His eyes went back to Faith. Gorgeous, sweet, sexy as sin Faith who hid her voluptuous body underneath her conservative attire. A virgin he was so close to claiming, to popping her cherry and owning her for life, but he fucked up. He tried so hard to get the new promotion and that dick screwed him. Didn't think he had enough experience and then when he raged, he had him thrown out of the company office building and then fired. It didn't help that he got drunk and fucked around with the blonde at the bar with Greg. Or that he got busted by Faith's cousin, and her friends.

He ran his hand along his unshaven beard. He screwed up big time. Was stuck in a rage when Faith broke things off with him. She wouldn't listen to his pleas for forgiveness. She wouldn't.

He slammed his fist down on the steering wheel and then took several uneasy breaths. He looked around him, seeing the patrol car coming down the street patrolling. He yanked up the clipboard and made it look like he pulled over to write some work things down. As the cop passed by he stared right at him and Andrew gave a nod and a smile. The cop looked at the clipboard and then gave a nod in return. *Right under your nose. Here I am watching that woman. For all you know, copper, I could be watching those kids, and getting ready to strike. You can't do a thing though. Not even if your gut clenches and you get a bad feeling. No, the bad guys have more rights than the good guys these days and I'm using that to my advantage.* He smirked and looked back across the playground as recess ended and Faith gathered her students.

She belonged to him. Her body was meant to be claimed by him and only him. Before he left for the job Greg hooked him up with, he had made sure she knew to never be with another man. To not look at another man or let another man touch her. Recently, though, her friends were getting involved with multiple men. Greg was pissed and worried that Everly would be doing that too and that he might lose her completely. Faith would never stray, for if she did then she would suffer greater than when he hurt her months ago. Whomever the guy was would die. End of story.

He felt the rage begin to simmer and he took several unsteady breaths. Andrew needed to remind himself that Faith wasn't seeing anyone, or going on dates, or even going out much. He needed to make his presence known and to help her understand that she belonged with him. It took months to get her to let him touch her intimately. There was no way she wasn't still a virgin. No way. He had a plan, and Faith was the prize to that plan coming together nicely.

* * * *

Faith Coleman looked at herself in the mirror. She smoothed her hands along the slim-fitting black skirt and then adjusted her breasts in the blue top she wore. It was a little more sexy than she would wear but tonight was special. Brook was going out as well as Emma and Casey. She buttoned the top up another button higher, helping her deep cleavage to disappear. The outfit was tight. She didn't want to draw attention to herself despite knowing that a certain manager at Gordon's would make a point of looking at her. His expressions were dark, but flirty. He would appear out of nowhere and press up against her back, move in and sweep her away when some guys were hitting on her and she looked scared. It was like he took a protective role over her and she didn't know why. He was older, and very handsome in a rugged, seasoned kind of way.

She turned sideways. Was she trying to look good for him? Trying to show an interest she wished she had the guts to have? She felt the tears fill her eyes. Andrew's words haunted her dreams, and apparently were forceful enough to be implanted in her head. *"You belong to me and only me. I screwed up, Faith, but I'll make it up to you. I'll be back. Don't ever let another man touch you or I'll kill him."*

She shivered from the memories. From the constant threats he made when she refused to see him and got the order of protection on him. She then moved from her cottage in Sussex to the town of Mercy when the cottage was for sale. She hadn't quite enough money but Brook loaned her what she needed and she paid her back. In fact, she owed one more payment to Brook and she would be sure to get that to her.

She shouldn't be going tonight. She was a bad judge of character and older men like Rocky were players. Men looking for sex and nothing more. As lonely as she felt, and attracted to the man, she wouldn't lose her virginity on meaningless sex.

She grabbed her purse, made sure everything was locked up and headed out to her car. Fifteen minutes later she was at Gordon's. Her friends greeted her hello and as she was handed her drink and reached for it, a strong, thick arm came around her waist just as two guys were passing by. She looked to the right, but then heard Rocky's voice.

"Just making sure they didn't bump into you, Miss Coleman," he said and she went numb with desire. The feel of his thick, large arm around her midsection made her feel feminine and safe. He was so charismatic, older, and sexy. He put the younger guys to shame and she wondered why she even found him attractive when he was obviously just out to mess with her and maybe get lucky.

She pulled from his hold. "Good evening, Mr. Gove. Busy night for you as usual, I see," she said very calmly. He looked her over and she felt it. Everywhere.

"Hi, Rocky." Two women came by. A blonde and a redhead. They eyed him over and the redhead licked her lips and stroked his arm. Faith was instantly turned off despite still feeling the attraction to the man. Rocky definitely grabbed women's attention. He looked like some NFL linebacker, was very tall, and with that gruff along his face he looked mean yet important. Like a person would be cool just by hanging out with him. Faith felt like a mouse. Like something that could be snapped in half by a man his size.

"Faith?" He whispered her name, reached up to touch her cheek and she snapped out of her daze, out of the angry, fearful expression she surely had and turned away. Thank God Emma directed a question toward her.

* * * *

Rocky was pleasantly surprised to see Faith here. He didn't know why he was so compelled to flirt with her and make that serious, yet shy, unapproachable demeanor of hers get to him as he took it as a challenge to affect her. He hadn't expected his game to affect him, but it did. In fact, every time Brook, Emma, Casey or one of her other friends came here with their men to hang out he would look for her. Rarely did she come, but tonight was special. Tonight Brook was back to visit, still recovering from her injuries. He felt that sick sensation in his gut. He completely understood Kinchley, Kernan, and Conan's protectiveness over Brook and the fears they had when she was taken. Brook had capabilities and training. A toughness that most women didn't have. Women like Faith surely didn't have and nor should she.

He stared at her now, the tight black skirt that went lower than most women her age would wear. It stopped right above the knees. Her top was slim-fitting, accentuating her tiny waist and full breasts but showed no cleavage. Again, most women would have at least kept the top buttons undone, showing off some of their racks. Not Faith. No, she wore hardly any makeup and didn't need, too. She was a natural beauty, and those eyes. Holy fuck, those baby blue eyes were what drew him in. Then add in the glasses, the shoulder length sophisticated style and how prim and proper she was and he was aroused. Hell, he fantasized about the games they could play in the bedroom. He wondered if she would be game for them and then felt like he committed a crime for thinking such dirty thoughts about a school teacher. Christ, he was forty fucking years old. Had slept with a lot of women over the years, and it wasn't until a couple of years ago that he slowed down, and was no longer interested in the one night stands. He wanted more, and he remained single, hadn't slept with any women despite having access to plenty. Then she walked into Gordon's one night with her friends and that was it. She was on his radar.

As he thought about his brothers Paulie and Hendrick, both retired Army Rangers and now members of SWAT in Castings, he wondered what they would have thought of her after meeting her when Brook was here one night. He noticed both of them keeping their eyes glued to her, but neither approached and both were swarmed by single women looking for sex. He hadn't asked them, and he wouldn't push anything. They were a few years younger, a bit more wild, still recovering from their experiences in the military and now in SWAT, and didn't seem ready to settle down.

His heart raced. "Settle down? What the fuck am I thinking?" he wondered and looked her over again. The swell of her nice, round ass, her petite figure, and how small she was compared to everyone around her. He felt protective, and he knew that a woman like Faith meant commitment, meant a future, and she would probably want a family, a house with the white picket fence, a dog in the yard and normal men. They weren't normal men. They were tough. Him included, despite now spending his days and nights as a manager of Gordon's. It kept his mind sane and away from the thoughts of nearly dying in war as well as losing Keith, their brother who died in a drunk driving accident.

He exhaled and squinted his eyes and looked back toward the bar. He didn't want to think about that. About the downhill path Keith was going on and that he, Paulie and Hendrick couldn't help him with. It was worse, knowing that the night Keith died his girlfriend at the time, Hailey, had told him she was pregnant. Baby Brianna was in Kindergarten.

Of course he and his brothers took care of Hailey and Brianna and helped out in any way they could. After all, that was their niece, their blood and Hailey was a special young woman who deserved happiness and not what Keith put her through.

He glanced at Faith one more time. She was perfect, but she was young and deserved a younger guy, and he knew that but he just couldn't seem to get her off his mind. He should though. A woman like Faith deserved a guy with a regular job, a regular past, and not one tainted by the violence of war, the tragedy of his brother's addiction, and the inability to commit. He was out of his head even thinking she would be attracted to him. Fifteen fucking years older. *Jesus, I need to get my head out of my ass.*

Chapter 1

"Miss Coleman. Miss Coleman, I dink my sagwich gave me a belly ache." Billy stood by Faith's desk, holding his belly and looking sad. She gave him a soft smile as the other children rested for ten minutes after recess.

He looked really pale and she scrunched her eyes together and told him to come closer. "What do you feel, Billy?"

"My head hurts, my belly's tight and rumbling. I'm hot," he said and she felt his forehead.

"Aw, baby, you're heating up." She could tell he had a fever, and she picked him up and let him lay his head on her shoulder as she called down to the office.

A few minutes later one of the office assistants brought Billy down to the nurse. She smiled as he gave her a weak smile. For a minute she thought about these children. About the classes she had before them and how much she wanted to have a family one day. There were a lot of fears, and it didn't seem like she was meeting anyone who was husband or father material. She was still young, twenty-five, and was pretty set in her life. This was her career, a school teacher, and she was making good money, had her own little house a block from the beach, and she could handle her finances. Her family was small. One brother who was in the service, and basically never returned home to New Jersey. He lived abroad and he took one assignment after the next. Her parents lived in New Jersey and were retired, going on trips out of the country and basically focused on themselves. She got tired of sitting around trying to establish roots when there was no one there to establish those roots with. Faith realized pretty quickly that she needed to learn to be alone, that no one stayed forever.

On a whim she applied for the teaching position online, drove down here, to South Carolina for the interview and got the job. She remembered being so shocked and then the panic set in. The fears of truly being on her own but she did it. She remembered standing there in her small apartment and it hit her. There was no one to call to celebrate her good news. No one to discuss options with. The decision was hers and hers alone. Her parents focused on themselves and her brother focused on himself, so why shouldn't she do the same?

She packed everything up from her apartment, drove down here with her car and her things, and found a place with help from Principal Margaret Hutch, her first friend in Mercy.

She met Brook and Emma only a couple of weeks later at a fundraising event and then they started hanging out at Corporal's. There, she got friendly with Kai, North, Amelia, April, Casey, Emma, and Afina, but Brook she was extra close to. Brook she considered a best friend, and she also came to her aid that one dreadful night.

She swallowed hard. She didn't hang out much but there was a bond there, and then when she was out one day shopping, she met Andrew. He seemed so perfect. He was a gentleman, and he was a soldier like the other men her friends hung out with. He was good-looking, sort of aggressive, which made up for her shyness. He took control so she didn't have to, and she accepted that. She was thrilled to finally meet a man and start dating. A man who made her feel like she was perfect, even though she felt she wasn't, and she wanted him to meet her friends. He refused to. He didn't want to meet them, and had become very overprotective of her. He was always working and trying to move up in the construction company he worked for. He was always complaining about the boss and how anti-American he was and how that boss had something against Andrew. It was a constant conversation between them and a sure indicator that something was going wrong. She ignored it because she wasn't a confrontational person and ultimately Andrew scared her. He had been in the military. He shared some stories of some things he did and some training he had. He even placed her into a hold one night to show her how weak and vulnerable she was. He never offered to teach her anything. It was like he wanted her to know that he was more powerful and it worked. He controlled her and she allowed it.

She swallowed hard as the children took their naps and rested from recess and tried not to think about Andrew or over a year ago. It was hard though. Especially at night when she was alone. There were so many signs that she should have accepted as warnings, but she didn't. Her self-esteem was low. She wasn't the kind of woman to flaunt her assets or to dress sexy to flirt with men or to make her boyfriend jealous. She didn't see herself as beautiful.

One night when they were out on a date, Andrew walked away to take a call because the bar was loud. She was sitting all alone and some guy approached and flirted. She told him she was with someone and he didn't listen. Things got out of hand quickly and Andrew lost it when he returned. He threatened the guy, and the guy gave him a shove and Andrew punched him. One hit, and the guy went down. Andrew grabbed her arm and ushered her out of there, hurting her, he was holding her so tight. When they got to his car he raged. He screamed at her and told her that she belonged to him and him only and if any other man touched her or she allowed another man to ever do that he would kill them. She was crying. She remembered it clearly, and she was mixed up, confused and uncertain what to do. Was this normal behavior for a boyfriend? Her gut clenched. Thank God she hadn't slept with him, but instead hugged him, apologized for what, she didn't know, and she calmed him down.

It was a smart move.

Her shyness was a negative attribute as far as she was concerned. It made her fearful of her judgment and all because of Andrew. Several months of dating and she nearly slept with him. How much she would have regretted that at this point. A year ago she was battered, bruised, and calling Brook for help. Then she was back to laying low, going out only here and there because she feared Andrew's return. She hadn't dated anyone. No one even asked her out. Well, not the right types of men anyway. She was blinded by her own insecurities and fears. She was a bad judge of character so it was better to not date at all. She was starting to think that something could be wrong with her. Her other friends were dating, and enjoying their twenties. Why couldn't she put Andrew behind her? Why was she afraid of every man she met who flirted or acted interested?

Her heart had been broken by Andrew despite not being intimate with him. He had been her first true boyfriend. He had manipulated her mind into thinking of how she needed to behave with a boyfriend and what was expected. She feared upsetting him so she walked on eggshells. Faith still was afraid. Afraid that he may return and cause her trouble, hurt her, force himself on her or even hurt her friends to get to her. She remembered his threats against other men. Perhaps in the back of her mind that was why she didn't date and why she found something wrong with every guy that asked her out. It was like she feared Andrew finding out and then hurting the guy.

It wasn't like she loved Andrew. She didn't hate him either and that was probably why she wanted to avoid violence. She was a good person and a forgiving person, but perhaps to a fault.

She sighed and got her mind back on the class and the last two hours of the day. It was a Friday and tonight she would relax with a bottle of wine and a nice, hot bubble bath. Her big Friday night plans? Tomorrow was a fundraising event in town hosted by Guardians of Hope and she told Kai she would help to run one of the tables, or do whatever was needed to assist. She loved helping out with anything having to do with raising money for first responders and Guardians of Hope. Not only because of her brother, but also because of the many parents she met who were part of such organizations as military, law enforcement, and firefighters. She knew the sacrifices they made and she supported them wholeheartedly.

Who knew where Kai might place her, so tonight she would relax and tomorrow be energized for whatever would come her way.

Chapter 2

"Thermo!" Kai reached back and removed his hand from her ass. They were behind the counter running the fifty-fifty raffles, and also signing in everyone who was volunteering. It was a bit chaotic this morning and she felt a little overwhelmed.

Thermo pressed up against her back and held her hips. He whispered next to her neck.

"You know I can't help but to cop a feel every chance I get. It's been non stop all morning," he complained and she couldn't help but to blush and lean back against him. She reached her hand up as she turned toward him and cupped his cheek.

"I feel it, too, Thermo, but there are a lot of people around and children, too, so watch those stray hands," she scolded and tapped his jaw. He narrowed his eyes at her and she almost felt intimidated. She was way past being fearful of Thermo, Selasi, and Zayn. As big and bad as they were, she knew they loved her and she loved them. She also knew what she could get away with.

"Oh, you just wait until later."

She giggled as Faith and Afina approached.

"Okay, boss, where do you need us?" Afina asked and Kai chuckled.

"Afina, you can stay here and help me with selling these raffles and Thermo can walk Faith over to the pavilion to assist Caden, Selasi and the guys getting donations for the fundraising dinner in two weeks and other donations," Kai said and both women smiled.

"I'll walk you over, Faith," Thermo said and Kai could see the fearful expression on Faith's face. She was intimidated. Kai couldn't blame her, Thermo was a sight.

* * * *

"Thanks for helping out," Thermo said to her and she nodded.

"No problem. I love all the work Kai does to help raise money for our first responders and military."

"She said you have a brother in the military, right?" he asked.

"Yes, he's very into it and I haven't seen him in a few years now."

"That's a long time," he said, seeming surprised.

"He's out of the country and in a high position now so he can't really leave."

"You should visit him then."

"I've thought about it but I teach summer classes for camp and the high school, too," she said and then heard her name.

"Miss Coleman!" She heard the little male voice and looked to see one of her students walking with his parents. He ran to her and hugged her leg. They had just gotten to the table where Caden was. Everyone was saying hello and the parents knew Caden and Thermo. She bent down to talk to Hank, the little boy from class.

"Hi, Hank, are you having fun?" she asked him.

"Yes I am. I seen a bunch of friends, too."

"Fantastic. I'm so glad that you're having fun," she said.

He scrunched his eyes at her and looked her over.

"Hey, you're not wearing a dress." He sounded like he was scolding her and she stood up just as Hank's father shook her hand hello, laughing at his son, and then he waved to someone behind her.

"Rocky, what the heck are you doing here?" Hank's dad said and she stepped to the side when Rocky appeared and reached over to shake the man's hand. Their gazes locked and Rocky gave her the once over, and then quickly turned away as Hank's mom greeted him, too.

"You smell good though so I guess it's okay," Hank added, hugging her again and they all chuckled. So did Faith.

She caressed Hank's hair. "I do wear other things besides dresses when I'm not working." She smoothed her hands down the short beige skort she wore and smiled at him. She had on a snug fitting T-back tank top with a white blouse over it.

"Say good-bye to Miss Coleman. We need to head to the car safety demonstration," his dad said and they waved good-bye. She started to turn toward Caden and the guys when Rocky slid his hand to her waist. She gasped and turned to look way up at him. In the tennis shoes she wore he really towered over her.

"What are you doing?" she asked him.

He inhaled. "Hmm, the kid was right, you smell really good," he teased, shocking her. She stepped from his light hold, pushed her glasses up a little, and moved toward the table and Caden. Caden squinted his eyes, seeming serious but then smiled at her.

"I'm here to help," she whispered, her voice sounding shaky to her own ears. Rocky intimidated her. Not only because of his extra large size, muscles and military background, but because he was a flirt, and was older by a lot of years, experienced with women and someone who didn't take women seriously at all. She didn't know why he teased her, or even spoke to her. In fact, she wondered why he would take a protective stance next to her or even look her way when models threw themselves at him.

"Thanks so much, Faith, we could use the help," Caden said.

"For the record, you look fantastic, don't know why the kid was giving you a hard time," some guy said to her and winked.

"Faith, meet Brian. Faith is a school teacher in Mercy Elementary," Caden said and smiled.

She shook Brian's hand and he held it a second longer than what would be considered normal.

"No school teacher looked like you when I was in elementary school," he said.

Before she could respond, Rocky was next to her, brushed by her shoulder and spoke to Brian.

"Like she hasn't heard that line before, kid? Move on. Don't you have some redhead to flirt with?"

"What do you mean?"

"The chick you were all over last night at Gordon's and the one you were making out with in the parking lot thirty minutes ago? Ring a bell?" he asked and Faith shook her head and then walked closer to Caden, who laughed.

"So what do you need for me to do?" she asked and Caden showed her the tickets to sell, that tables could be reserved, as well, but money up front, not at the door. She gathered the tickets, a pen and some change and then walked over toward the other end of the table. She could hear the conversation going on behind her.

"What the hell, Rocky, you trying to sabotage my chances with the Kindergarten teacher? She's so hot, and is single. Everyone knows it."

"Leave her alone and show some respect. She has class. Don't make me warn you again."

"Holy shit," Brian said and then walked away.

"What?" she heard Rocky say to Caden and she turned to glance over her shoulder. The two men stared at one another and then Caden snickered.

"I'll be damned. Good luck," Caden said and she didn't know why but then some guys with Mercy police T-shirts approached.

"Hey, gorgeous, is this where we buy the tickets for the dinner in two weeks?" one blond asked. He gave her a wink and eyed her over, along with his four buddies.

"Yes it is. Will you be buying single tickets or a whole table? It's about twenty dollars cheaper if you buy a table of ten."

"We could get ten guys to come," one of the guys said and smiled at her.

"Or some dates," another one chimed in.

"Are you going to be there?" the blond asked her.

"I'm not sure. So how many tickets?" she asked and they said they would buy a table and then guys chipped in and then she handed them their tickets and wrote down their names for a full table of ten.

"Just make sure your friends bring those tickets with them, okay?" she asked.

"What's your name, honey?"

"Faith."

One whistled. "Gorgeous name. Will you be my date that night?" the guy asked and his buddies moaned.

She laughed. "No thank you."

"Why not?" he pushed.

She swallowed hard and then looked away then back at him.

"I have a date already."

"Damn. Should have known." They walked away and she waited and then another set of guys came over, flirting and buying tickets and then some women came over and they wanted to know if hot guys would be there. She had to laugh, they weren't much younger than her. She wished she could be so brazen and take a chance but she knew she would screw up and choose the wrong guy. She was better off alone. It wasn't worth the heartache when things failed.

* * * *

Rocky kept his eyes on Faith. It was difficult to not remain staring at her and checking out her body, inhaling her perfume or catch a glimpse of the deep cleavage of her breasts when her blouse blew open in a slow breeze. She was petite, sexy, yet conservative and seemed to be trying to hide her full breasts. Somehow it made her even sexier. She had an adorable laugh, a really sweet smile, and a sophistication about her, as well. Between that blonde shoulder length hair and those designer eyeglasses she looked intelligent, sweet and sexy.

He didn't know why he kept teasing her and flirting with her. She was too young for him, but shit, he would be lying if he said he wouldn't jump at an opportunity to get to know her more intimately. He didn't take women seriously though. Didn't date at all, and looked at women as a means to satisfy urges when they became too much. Even that wasn't a regular occurrence. He also wasn't an asshole, and he wouldn't play games with a woman so young and sweet as Faith, and someone who was such good friends with his friends.

He leaned back against the table with his arms crossed in front of his chest, and watched the multiple men that approached the table and even a few women. The women on the hunt for men in uniforms and the guys on the hunt for Faith. She let them down easy, in fact like a pro who regularly turned down dates and it made him wonder why. Some pretty decent guys her own age approached and could be a good fit. The thought brought on a surge of jealousy he hadn't expected.

When he saw his brothers Paulie and Hendrick approach with a few friends from SWAT he was shocked when their eyes landed on Faith. Paulie got straight-faced, and Hendrick crossed his arms in front of his chest as their buddies flirted with Faith. When it was their turn to purchase tickets Rocky moved in behind her, placed his hands on her shoulders and felt her tighten up.

"Meet my brothers, Paulie and Hendrick," he said and watched them closely. Paulie reached his hand out for her to shake, his eyes never leaving hers. He didn't even really check out her body, his focus was on her lips. That meant something. Then Hendrick gave a nod.

"Nice to meet you. So, did you want to buy tickets to the fundraising dinner?" she asked, then lowered her eyes to the table and tapped the ticket stack as if they were making her nervous.

"Yes. We'll take two. Well, Rocky, did you get yours yet?" Paulie asked.

"I'll buy it from Faith when we're all done here," he said and eased his hands from her shoulders and stood beside her. He locked gazes with Paulie and Paulie squinted as Hendrick paid her. That's when someone came up behind them and slammed into Faith. She fell against the table, and Rocky looked and saw it was a little kid. She turned to look and he was about to yell when he saw the boy was holding his throat and unable to talk.

"Johnny, are you choking?" she yelled at him and he nodded. She turned him around, wrapped her arms around his midsection and did the Heimlich maneuver. He heard a woman screaming and then who he thought were the parents coming over when the piece of chicken dislodged from his throat. The little boy was crying, Faith was on her knees on the ground as he hugged her and sobbed.

"Oh my God, Miss Coleman. Thank you so much. Oh God, he ran right to you. He saw you and he was choking and ran so fast to you," the mother carried on and was caressing his hair.

Faith pulled back and smoothed the boy's hair from his cheeks as some paramedics who were there today in case of an emergency approached.

"Are you okay now, Johnny?" Tears streamed down his cheeks, and he rubbed snot on her shirt from his nose and she didn't even care. Rocky couldn't believe it and when he looked at Paulie and Hendrick it seemed they were thinking the same thing.

"Let the nice paramedics check you out as a precaution, okay, Johnny? You're all right," Faith said and the paramedics walked with him as his mom hugged Faith and then his dad, too.

"You are above and beyond just a teacher, Faith. Thank you," he said and walked away.

She closed her eyes and exhaled and Rocky placed his hand on her shoulder and Paulie placed his hand on her hip.

"Are you okay?" they both asked and her eyes popped open.

She started to move away when Paulie stopped her. "I think you need to change your blouse," he said and she looked down and then made a funny face, before she pulled it off. Rocky's eyes zeroed in on her voluptuous figure as Caden approached.

"You are something else, Faith. Thank God you were here. I was heading over to tell you your replacements are here," he said and there were Casey, Ranger, and Roman.

Casey hugged Faith hello and then she said she was going to try and rinse off her blouse.

"Take a lunch break and enjoy the festivities. We're all good from here on out," Caden said and then gave her a wink.

She smiled.

"Why don't we walk with you? We just finished up at the booth we were working at and were going to grab some lunch. Come along with us," Paulie said.

She shyly pushed a strand of hair behind her ear, revealing tiny diamond stud earrings. Feminine and petite like her.

"Come on, it will be fun and there's no need to walk around alone," Paulie added and she nodded and they started walking.

"I need to find a restroom so I can clean this," she said to them.

"It's getting pretty hot out, I doubt you'll need it but we can find one," Rocky said.

She stared up at him and then looked at Hendrick and Paulie. "You guys are very tall, very big men. How tall are you actually?" she asked as they walked.

"Six feet four," Rocky told her, but then placed his hand on her hip as if guiding her.

She tightened up immediately. She was definitely on edge around them. It was different than most women. They threw themselves at him and his brothers. Hung on their arms and complimented their muscles. Damn, when he thought about the women he wasted time with he suddenly felt like he wasn't good enough for someone as classy, sophisticated and beautiful as Faith. She was shy, prim and proper yet sexy at the same time. He could only imagine how submissive of a lover she was. Maybe even inexperienced. He felt jealous of any other man that got to see her naked. Got to explore her with his mouth and make her come.

"Rocky." She said his name and he hadn't even realized that they were already by the building where the restrooms were.

He released his hold on her hip and gave her a smile. "We'll wait for you."

She gulped then looked at his brothers, who weren't so close.

"There's no need to. I think I'll just walk around a little and then head home."

He scrunched his eyes together. "Head home? Why? It's a nice day out, and there's a bunch to see. You don't like to socialize or something?" he asked and gave her the once-over. Could this be an act? He'd seen all different kinds of angles by women in his forty years of life.

She worried her bottom lip and glanced up at them again. "I socialize plenty, I just don't know you or your brothers and I don't make it a habit of just hanging out with men I don't know."

"Are you serious?" Paulie asked her. Now he looked at her like she was up to something.

"Your friends know us. We'll probably head over to where they are hanging out. I heard that Brook was going to be here. You're good friends with her, aren't you?" he asked and wondered why he felt like he was preying on the weak with her. She was incredibly gorgeous. The way she stood there, her head tilted back and trying to look up at him. Those baby blue eyes so telling, and that hairstyle was perfect for her, it also made her neck accessible and he would love to take a little taste. Holy fuck. He was losing his mind. He never looked at a woman and thought about her neck, and what she would taste like and smell like. What the fuck?

"Just do what you need to do and we'll wait here," he ordered. Her eyes widened and she quickly headed into the building.

"Jesus, Rocky, you losing your fucking touch or what?" Paulie asked him.

"Why are you even bothering? She's scared shitless of you, and us, and she's good friends with Brook. You don't need that kind of heat," Hendrick said to him.

He had an angry look on his face and he knew it. He could feel his body tighten and his mind go into a thousand directions but kept coming back to wanting to get to know Faith.

"Look at her. Don't fucking tell me that you feel nothing. The both of you immediately zeroed in on her when you came to the ticket table."

"She's a looker, but not typical," Paulie stated.

"Not an easy lay. That is a woman with class. A fucking school teacher. Why the fuck would she be interested in three hardcore soldiers, two currently active in SWAT?" Hendrick said to them.

"I'm not sure she is interested but I think I want to make her interested." Paulie gave a nod toward the door and as they all looked over she was coming out, and a guy held the door open for her, smiled, winked and then stared at her ass as she walked. The three of them must have had scowls on their faces because the poor woman stopped, eyes wide and held on to her blouse tight. Paulie cleared his throat.

"I saw Kinchley earlier and he said his brothers and Brook would be near the pavilion at lunch time. Why don't we head that way and see if they're there," he said to her.

She stared at him and Rocky watched as Paulie reached out and stroked her jaw.

"Sweetie, please stop looking at me like I'm a serial killer. I swear, you're safe with us," he said to her.

She pursed her lips and exhaled. "I don't think you're serial killers."

"Could have fooled me," Hendrick said as they started walking.

"I'm sorry. I don't mean to insult you. I…I just prefer to do things alone."

"What fun is that?" Rocky asked her, taking position on one side of her as Paulie took position on her other side and Hendrick remained behind her.

She didn't respond and they remained quiet until they got to the pavilion and she saw Brook. Brook's eyes widened and then she scrunched them together and gave Rocky the stare down. He knew in that moment that he and his brothers needed to decide what their intentions were with Faith. He didn't think he was commitment material, yet he wanted Faith all to himself and his brothers. Kind of not the way a commitment worked. He was older, too. Perhaps he needed to push this attraction aside. Faith deserved better. Hendrick was right.

* * * *

"What are you doing hanging out with Rocky, Paulie, and Hendrick?" Brook asked her as they sat by the picnic tables waiting for the guys to bring back food for them.

She explained about Rocky teasing her and then helping at the table too and then about little Johnny choking.

"Oh my God, that is crazy. Thank God you were there."

"I think he saw me and just ran to me to help him."

"Because he knew you would. Your kids love you."

"I love the kids. I truly love being a teacher," Faith said and smiled as she looked around at all the families enjoying the day.

"Apparently you have gained the attention of three pretty intense men. I'm not sure how I feel about this," Brook said.

"How you feel? I don't know what to think. Maybe they're just being nice, or worse, maybe they think I'm gullible."

"Gullible? Are we back to this again? I thought you were starting to gain more self-confidence? What happened to the self-defense classes you were starting?"

"Nothing works with my schedule."

"Bullshit. I don't know why you can't take the classes with the instructors I recommended. Corey said he would work around your schedule and even do nights."

"I don't feel comfortable with it. I'm not an aggressive person. That's why I wound up in the trouble I did."

"That isn't true. Andrew was an asshole and he took advantage of your timidness and used his muscles and his demands to force you to remain involved with him. He was abusive and if he didn't strike that night it would have happened another night instead."

"I know that, and it's something I need to live with."

"Well, don't let it hold you back from gaining more self-confidence. You haven't gone out with any guys since and that's over a year now. Maybe hanging out with Rocky and his brothers as friends first could be a positive thing."

"Brook, are you nuts?" she asked, eyes wide and then glanced behind her to make sure the men weren't coming back yet. "They are huge and like six feet four. I'm five feet three. They could toss me around with one arm and without even trying, and that isn't even touching their other capabilities as soldiers, and SWAT."

"They are good men and not batterers. I think it's kind of sexy that you're so petite and they are so big. You would definitely be protected between them."

"Controlled is more like it," Faith said and exhaled as she stared at her fingers on her lap.

"Controlled?"

Faith looked at her and whispered, "Rocky orders when he speaks. He scares me. Paulie does too with all those muscles and the way I felt so much when he touched my jaw and accused me of thinking he was a serial killer."

Brook laughed.

"Not funny. And Hendrick? Look at him. He is fierce, doesn't smile and he barely spoke to me since we met up with you guys."

"Well, I get the feeling that you aren't the only one who is shocked at the attraction between the four of you."

"I don't know. I think they're perfect, and I'm not. I'm just not a good judge of character, Brook. Plus I'm embarrassed about what Andrew did to me. I'm not over the fear of him and that's not fair to any man I would consider even having an interest in. Besides that, I don't know how to act. I don't know what a girlfriend is supposed to do or be like."

Brook sighed. "I think you're overthinking and the best thing to do would be to just go with the flow."

"I'm a school teacher. We don't go with the flow. I'm organized, everything has a time and a place to avoid chaos."

"Well, honey, take it from me, sometimes chaos is good. Sometimes it's hot," she said and winked.

"Oh God," Faith said and then Brook chuckled as the men appeared and were heading toward them.

As they all gathered around and set up their lunch to eat, the conversation flowed nicely. Faith just listened as the men talked about some upcoming events and then they mentioned some guy they all knew who was joining the Y in Mercy and teaching a combination of self-defense and kickboxing. She listened to them talk about the importance of having some form of self-defense and training. Faith totally felt uncomfortable. Everyone there was involved in the military or law enforcement or both. It made her feel like she was lame and weak to not even be able to defend herself if there were a situation.

"Do you take any classes, Faith?" Conan asked her. She shook her head. Immediately she noticed the expressions on Rocky, Paulie, and Hendrick's faces change. They seemed disappointed and angry.

"I can't believe you haven't taken any. Not even one?" Paulie asked.

"I was taking a self-defense class with Brook's friend Corey, but it really didn't work around my schedule," she said, feeling like she needed to defend herself.

"Listen, some people aren't that comfortable with the entire way self-defense classes are run," Brook said in her defense and Faith cleared her throat.

"I have a very busy schedule and my friends all have their own private training now. I just haven't found a place I'm comfortable with," she said.

She looked at Brook when the men basically went on to a different conversation, making it obvious that her excuse was lame. Now Faith felt like she needed to try and fit in some kind of self-defense class. Maybe she would. These guys thought she was weak and unable to handle things on her own. Well, they didn't know what she went through.

Just then she saw the guys from earlier in the day, the ones Caden told her about after they came to the table to flirt with her. They supposedly helped out with some sort of self-defense program as subs at the Y and were having an open house tomorrow.

"Excuse me a moment," she said and stood up. She walked over to the three men and stopped them. They of course smiled wide and she knew they would think she was flirting so she made sure they understood she meant business.

They looked past her and she didn't want to look, too, having a feeling that the men with Brook would think she was out of her mind.

"That open house is tomorrow, right?" she asked and the one blond smiled wide. He looked her over.

"You interested?" he asked.

"In learning self-defense," she said firmly.

"Of course. That's what we'll be teaching. Get there a little early and we can start some moves," the other guy said.

She had an uneasy feeling. Why was she over here? How come Paulie, Rocky, and Hendrick's response to her never taking self-defense got under her skin and made her react? She nibbled her bottom lip. The blond placed his hand on her shoulder and lowered slightly to look her in the eyes.

"Don't worry, sweetie, we'll go slow with you and teach you step-by-step instruction. Just show up so we know how serious you are in learning," he added.

She nodded, said thank you then walked back to the table.

"What was that all about?" Rocky asked her with attitude.

"Nothing," she said and went to sit down, which was basically right next to him.

"Nothing, my ass. What did you say to them?" he pushed.

"I just remembered what they said about teaching an open house tomorrow at the Y when they came by our table earlier. They invited me but I declined. Since you all looked at me like I was nuts for not having some form of self-defense training, I decided I would take them up on their offer."

"What?" Paulie asked, teeth clenched.

"They said they would take their time and go slow. Maybe that's what I need," she said and then took a sip of her iced tea.

"You're not going," Paulie stated.

Brook chuckled and Faith didn't know why. She looked at Paulie. "What are you talking about?"

"You aren't going," Hendrick stated but didn't look at her. Faith glanced at Brook's men, who looked half ready to reprimand her too and half about to smile.

Rocky turned in his seat and grabbed her by her shoulders.

"You are not going. It isn't happening," he stated firmly.

"Says who?" she asked.

"Me." Before she could ask Rocky what he was talking about, he kissed her. Right there, right in front of everyone he kissed her. She couldn't believe the instant attraction she had and how turned on she was that this extra large, older man just basically shut her up by kissing her, and it didn't seem like he wanted to stop either. Neither did she as she grabbed on to his shoulders, ran her hand up into his hair as he dipped her slightly and moaned into her mouth.

When they heard some hoots and hollers it brought them both back to the present and he pulled her back up and slowly released her lips. He stared into her face, which had to be flushed and he narrowed his eyes at her.

"Tomorrow morning Hendrick will be teaching you some self-defense skills. Not those guys and not at the Y. Understood?" he asked firmly.

"Not exactly," she whispered and the guys all started to laugh.

Rocky gripped her chin and cheek. "My brothers and I will explain. Thoroughly so you get it." He gave her a wink and then turned back around and started to finish eating his sandwich. She looked at Hendrick, who somehow seemed more serious than earlier and then to

Paulie, who licked his lips and gave her body the once over, making her nipples harden and her pussy actually clench. Holy shit. She liked the three of them. Rocky was staking some sort of claim. Was this a ménage? The start of one? They wanted sex?

"Oh God," she said and exhaled.

"Easy, Faith. Take your time and don't let those three hard asses freak you out. It will work out fine," Brook said but Faith wasn't sure about that at all.

Chapter 3

"I need to wrap things up. I want to get to my life, to fixing everything," Andrew said to Greg over the phone.

"Well, you can't yet. There's been a change of plans. Some guys of Leonard's were asking some questions about you and where you were staying. Apparently your little gift to his wife has sent him into a frenzy. I told you that was a bad fucking idea."

"He can't prove it was me. Besides that, it gives us more time to fuck with the company and start making those accidents happen on the construction sites. He'll be caught up in fines, shut down for placing workers in danger and paying out the ass while we sit back laughing. I already have plans in motion for three of the sites across the state."

"I'm telling you to slow down. You can't make these things happen so close together. It will alert the cops, hell, even the feds onto this. The plan is to make it look like he's a scumbag."

"He is a scumbag. How fucking long before I can make the other shit happen?"

"Give it a couple of weeks, then a few more weeks in between the next one."

"What? No, no fucking way. I want to see Faith. I need to make things up to her and start working on getting her back."

"You need to be careful with that, too. You have no patience when it comes to her. She isn't dating anyone. Everly told me when I called her this morning."

"You're talking to her? I thought she was mad at you."

"She still is but the attraction is there and she knows it," Greg said.

"It isn't fair. I need Faith. I'm doing all of this for her. To prove to her that I would do anything for her."

"Call her instead. Start getting her used to your voice, you caring about her and talking things out."

"I sent her something. She should get it today."

"What did you send her?"

"Purple roses."

"Nice, but will she accept them? I would have started calling her first."

"She will. I gave her purple roses on our first date and then sporadically here and there to surprise her. She'll get it and accept them, and I'll start working on calling her and getting back involved with her life."

"Good, stay where you are and wait another two weeks before you do the next set up. I'll take care of things here and internally in the company."

Andrew ended the call and leaned back on the bed. He lay there in the hotel just thinking about Faith and all the things he planned on doing with her. His sweet, caring school teacher would take him back. She would forgive him because she had such a great big heart. She was controllable, easily manipulated and she needed his protection. Any guy or guys could come along and take her from him. Make him lose his chance to be with her again. He had to make sure she didn't stray.

He glanced at his watch. *Tomorrow I'll call her. Tomorrow I'll start getting into her head and reminding her about who she belongs to and about coming back into her life. Tomorrow.*

* * * *

Paulie took Faith's hand, stopping her by the building. They were all going to meet at the center for the police car races. They had a mock track set up in the parking lot with safety cones the officers had to maneuver around. It was a demonstration showing the local law enforcement training and capabilities in the police cruisers.

She stopped and looked way up at Paulie. He stepped closer, slid his arm around her waist and hoisted her against him.

"Paulie."

He shook his head. Stared down into her eyes, so blue and stunning, and with the glasses she wore they stood out even more. He felt so much as he stroked her jaw and gripped her chin.

"You came out of nowhere and shocked the shit out of us. I feel so protective of you, Faith. It's like you need looking after." She went to shake her head.

"You do need looking after. What the hell were you thinking going over to those guys and saying you would go to their self-defense training tomorrow? You knew they were flirting with you earlier," Rocky reprimanded.

"You made me do it," she said, glancing at Rocky and Hendrick, who were right there.

Paulie widened his eyes. "It's our fault you flirted back and now they think they have a chance with you?" Paulie asked.

"I wasn't flirting back. I accepted the invitation to try their class. That's what you were all hinting at, wasn't it? For me to get some kind of training?" she asked.

"Is she serious?" Hendrick asked.

"You're too damn sweet," Rocky stated, sounding frustrated.

"I bet she tastes sweet, too," Paulie said and then pressed his lips to hers. When he kissed her she was shocked that she felt the same deep attraction she had with Rocky. This was insane and she could feel her body shaking and her mind couldn't even process what was happening here. When she felt the second set of hands on her hips from behind and then lips against her neck, she moaned into Paulie's mouth. It was Hendrick and then Rocky joined in and ran a hand along her waist under her top and against her belly. She pulled back from Paulie's touch and pushed Rocky's hand down and off of her, but then Hendrick turned her around and stopped kissing her neck to kiss her lips. He ravaged her mouth, squeezed her ass and pressed her hard against his body. She felt his thick, hard cock and it both scared her and aroused her. She never felt so instantly turned on and wanton. Holy God, she felt like she could have sex with these men. Like she could give up her virginity. She pressed her hands against his chest and he eased back slowly.

"Easy now, darling. God damn, you pack one hell of a punch for a pint size thing," he said and winked at her.

"What have we done?" she asked and reached up to press her fingertips to her swollen, wet lips. Her breasts felt swollen and needy and her panties were wet.

"Got things started, Faith," Hendrick said to her and she shook her head and started to step back and away from them.

Rocky slid his arm around her waist. "Whoa, slow down, no need to panic," he said.

She stared up at him. Absorbed the feel of his big, muscular arm around her waist and then at all those muscles, that fierce expression. Then she looked at Hendrick and Paulie, who sported similar looks. They were big, capable, and could seriously cause her harm.

"My God, you're shaking. Please don't be scared. Fuck," Rocky said and pulled her into his arms and hugged her tight. He caressed her back and she was lost in his arms. She gripped on to his sides and to his shirt.

"Oh God, this can't be happening. I can't allow this. It isn't right. Why are you doing this to me? What is it you want? Is this a game? Very funny, the joke is over," she said and pulled away from Rocky and fixed her glasses and then smoothed her hands along her hips. She gasped when Hendrick gripped her hips, slid his hands along her belly and hugged her from behind. His mouth was pressed against her neck and by her ear.

"Slow down and breathe. God damn, you're so shy and sweet. We didn't mean to scare you or overwhelm you, Faith," he said and she exhaled.

"You did," she whispered and Paulie and Rocky stood in front of her, eyed her over and then Hendrick eased back. He held her hand, brought it to his lips and she watched him kiss her knuckles. Those bold blue eyes of his were locked on to her and the fierce expression remained.

"How about we head over to the parking lot and the course to watch?" Rocky suggested.

She was stunned at what just took place and at the wild thoughts running through her head. She nodded and they walked. Hendrick remained holding her hand and Paulie and Rocky were right there with her. She pulled her hand away from him and rubbed her hands together. She was completely freaking out here. This wasn't good. They were older, very attractive men and they could get any woman they wanted, why the hell were they kissing her, touching her and making moves on her?

She stopped short. Her hands were on her hips and they stopped to look at her.

"What is it you're after?" she asked them as anger pooled in her belly. She wasn't a game. She couldn't let the fact that they were dominant and sexy overrule rational thought here.

"What do you mean?" Paulie asked her but Hendrick and Rocky crossed their arms in front of their chests and stared down at her. If that wasn't intimidation then she didn't know shit about it.

She exhaled, eyed him over in his navy blue SWAT T-shirt and the dark black camo pants. No words came out of her mouth. She was too busy drooling over Paulie and forgot what she said. It didn't help that he bent slightly as he held her arms and squinted in a cute way that made her heart race.

"We aren't after anything. We like you, and we're getting to know you. Now let's enjoy the event and then talk some more."

The sound of sirens wailing alerted them that the event was starting out and ended the discussion. She was confused, unsure but as they walked her over to the fence for a closer look then formed a semicircle around her, protecting her from anyone bumping into her, she began to enjoy the sensations and let her mind wander.

It was hard to concentrate on the vehicles speeding through the obstacle courses while Paulie, Hendrick, and Rocky took every opportunity to caress her skin, to even whisper into her ear little descriptions of techniques as if she cared. She didn't even absorb what she was watching, she absorbed what she was feeling. When the one police car skidded along the parking lot looking as if it was coming close to the fence, she stepped back. Rocky's arm went around her waist and then his mouth was against her neck and shoulder. "You're safe with us," he said and she leaned back, tilted to the right, giving him better access to her neck and a sensitive spot he kept finding. Her eyes locked on to Hendrick's. He brought her hand to his lips and kissed her knuckles. She was in serious trouble here.

When Paulie began to caress under her hair and neck after Rocky released his hold and her lips, she couldn't believe how turned on she was and how much she enjoyed their touches. Could she actually entertain such an attraction or was she asking for nothing but a broken heart and problems?

As the crowd began to cheer she pulled forward and clapped, as well, although she missed most of the event. Paulie took her hand and led her away with the crowd and his brothers.

"So, what time works for you tomorrow to meet up at our place?" he asked her. She pulled her hand back.

"What?" she asked, hand over her heart. Rocky laughed and pressed his palm to her hip.

"For the self-defense training. We have a built-in gym and an area for sparring and training," Rocky told her.

Paulie reached out and stroked her jaw. "Get that mind out of the gutter, baby, unless you want to skip the dating process and go right to bed," he said.

She shook her head and pulled away, took a few steps back and looked away from them.

"I don't know if this will work."

"Hey, they're just teasing," Hendrick sort of snapped at her. Or maybe that was just Hendrick's normal tone of voice. She wasn't sure. She reacted.

"Is that what they're doing?" she whispered.

"Damn," Paulie said and pulled her into his arms and kissed her again. She was shocked and caught off guard at his actions. Why did he keep doing this to her? As he plunged his tongue deeper in exploration and then she felt his hand over her ass, she squeezed his arms and moaned into his mouth. He released her lips slowly.

"You are so damn shy and sexy. I can't take it," he admitted.

"Don't do that."

"Do what?" he asked.

"Just kiss me to shut me up or to control me."

"What? That isn't why I kissed you. I like you a lot. Your innocent, timid expressions do me in, sweetie." He stroked her cheek and she didn't know if she could believe him or not. It was all so confusing and fast paced.

"You need to slow down. You're moving too fast," she said to him and he placed his hands on his hips and squinted at her like she was crazy.

"We'll try, but no promises," Rocky told her.

"So what time tomorrow?" Hendrick chimed in, straight faced. She felt like she pissed him off somehow. He was quite demanding too and maybe he expected her to be like other women and just throw herself at them and let them lead her. The thought brought on a tingling sensation of desire. Holy shit, this was a first. She didn't want to go slow either but knew she had to.

"I need slow."

"You mentioned that. So what time tomorrow for training?" Paulie said to her.

"Eleven good or earlier? Then we can do lunch afterward. Maybe take a swim in the pool," Hendrick suggested. The three men looked her over as if they were imagining her in her bikini. Oh God.

"Is that what you normally do after training women?" she asked with attitude she didn't know where from. They widened their eyes.

"I don't do private lessons. Been asked, but never did them," he told her. Was that supposed to make her desire him more? Make her feel special? Or like he was giving her the lessons to ease her mind before he went in for the kill? Jesus, she was freaking out big time.

"I guess eleven, and then we'll see about swimming. I usually catch up on things at home and doing yard work."

"Where do you live?"

"Eastside."

"We live on Coastal."

"In one of those big houses?" she asked, surprised.

"I can pick you up so you won't get lost. I'll be by at 10:45," Hendrick told her.

"Let's exchange phone numbers and then you can text your address," Paulie said and pulled out his cell phone. They were moving so quickly and she just reacted, obeyed and felt comfortable with them.

"Okay, I should get going."

"What? It's early," Paulie added.

"I have a lot to do today, including food shopping for the week."

They stared at her.

"We'll walk you to your car." As they did they stopped her here and there and kissed her. It was as if they really didn't want her to leave, or for the day to end and by the time they got to her car, she was feeling it, too. As she turned toward Rocky to tell them she enjoyed the day and would see them tomorrow, he grabbed her around the waist, pulled her into his arms and kissed her with vigor and purpose. She kissed him back, gripped on to his sides as he ran one hand under her hair and neck, holding her in place while devouring her moans and then his other hand squeezed her ass. He moaned into her mouth and then eased his mouth off her lips and then went to her neck. As he readjusted his position she ran her hands up his chest and hugged him. He bent lower, lifted her up and twirled her around.

"God damn, baby, I want to take you home and explore every inch of this sexy body with my brothers, but I know that's way too fast for you."

She tightened up as he lowered her feet to the ground. When she eased back, all three men licked their lips.

"Jesus, look at her," Hendrick whispered. Paulie reached out and stroked her cheek and then down her top over her breast. The nipple hardened and she stepped back, lowering her head.

"Tomorrow can't come fast enough," Paulie said and she gave a little wave as she got into her car and they stepped back, just watching her. Holy shit, were they gorgeous men. Real men, seasoned, experienced, oh so very experienced. *My God, I want them. I want to take this chance. I might have a heart attack, but what a hell of a way to die. Holy heavens.*

* * * *

"Holy shit, how the fuck did this happen. Did you see her? See that expression, that fucking body she hides, her shyness, and reaction to us? Holy shit," Paulie said and ran his fingers through his hair.

"I know, she looked so sweet and innocent. Definitely not as experienced as us. Holy fuck, I feel like I'm committing a crime. Is robbing the fucking cradle a crime?" Rocky asked as they chuckled at him and started walking back.

"When I kiss her I don't think about how fucking young she is, I think about the curves, the way she feels and smells. She smells so fucking good," Hendrick added.

"I know. It's funny because when we were at the table this morning and this little boy from her class spotted her and ran to hug her, he was surpised she wasn't wearing a dress but said she still smelled as good as she does at school and he hugged her leg again."

Paulie chuckled.

"Jesus, I just felt jealous over a little kid hugging her leg and inhaling her scent," Hendrick said and they laughed more.

"This is incredible. We haven't talked about this idea. About sharing a woman in quite some time," Rocky said, feeling that uneasy feeling begin to simmer.

"We don't know what this is yet. We shouldn't jump the gun and get all serious and start picking out fucking china," Hendrick snapped.

Rocky knew there were going to be some hard feelings, a lot of emotions. They had planned to share a women with Keith if they found one they all were attracted to and wanted that with. He hadn't told them about Hailey, and it was too late when they realized he had such a bad drinking problem and then died.

"Listen, we'll work it out. It's a good thing that Faith needs slow. We don't need to rush into this and then screw it up," Paulie added.

"Definitely not. We need to be sure because our good friends, men you and I work with and are around all the time, are dating her girlfriends," Rocky said to them.

"We need to find out more about her. How old is she really? How many lovers has she had?" Paulie asked.

"What? Why the fuck do you want to know that?" Hendrick asked.

"I think she hasn't had many, and after kissing her and seeing her reaction, it wouldn't surprise me if she hasn't had one."

"A virgin, Paulie? Seriously?" Hendrick asked but then looked at Rocky and squinted and then looked back at Paulie. Rocky widened his eyes.

"Great, Now not only do I feel fucking old, but like some dick for wanting that from her. To be her first and only. Holy fuck, if she is, she's ours. All ours and no one else's. Do you guys get that?" He ran his hand along his beard and then exhaled. "Let's not assume anything."

"So putting a tracking device on her ankle and claiming her our woman, making sure every man knows to stay away from her, is probably a bit too crazy of an idea?" Hendrick asked. Paulie and Rocky laughed.

"She'll take back her apology thinking that you're a serial killer."

Hendrick snorted. "What the fuck. How can some pint size sexy little bombshell do this to us? I did not see this shit coming when I got up this morning," Paulie said.

"Just wait until you get to roll around on the mats with her tomorrow, Hendrick, and how me and Paulie join in, as well," Rocky said.

"Tomorrow can't come fast enough," Hendrick said and they all agreed.

Chapter 4

Faith was smiling wide as she drove to her house. She was already thinking about what to wear tomorrow to her first self-defense class with Hendrick. Oh boy, Hendrick was intense and he had such big muscles, too. She knew what would happen. They would wind up making out on the mats and maybe not doing much learning. She should make sure he was serious and taught her things. She needed to learn and she didn't want them thinking she was weak. She didn't like how it felt when they thought she had no training and was basically stupid for not having any. They were right in a way because women were more often than not targets for violence and crimes. It could give her an upper hand.

As she pulled down her street and thought about what bathing suit to wear, she spotted a van by her house but a guy holding some flowers at her neighbor's house. Then her neighbor pointed at her. She wondered what was going on and pulled into her driveway to park when the flower delivery guy approached. The package was wrapped up in purple tissue paper.

"Miss Coleman?" he asked.

"That's me."

He smiled wide. "Great, these are for you. I was going to leave them with the neighbor and then leave a note for you."

"Glad I got here in time," she said and then reached into her purse and pulled out two dollars to give him. She then headed into her house as he drove away. She wondered who would send her flowers. As she locked the door and then set her things down on the small island in the kitchen she looked at the package. She undid the wrapping and as the purple roses came into view she felt as if her heart stopped beating.

She stepped back, covered her mouth as thoughts and emotions flooded her body. The instant fear, the meaning behind the purple roses and who they came from.

"It can't be from him. They can't be. Why now?" she wondered, thinking aloud about meeting Rocky, Paulie, and Hendrick and liking them, letting them kiss her, touch her and make plans with her. Did Andrew know? Was he watching her somehow? The panicked feeling began to start and as she looked at the card attached to the gorgeous purple roses she reached up and took it.

"My dearest Faith. I am so very sorry for what I did. I plan on making it up to you. Please forgive me. Andrew."

She closed her eyes and remembered the night he struck. How angry at his boss he was and how he took it out on her. She called Brook right away. Refused to press charges because she was so afraid of him but also felt like he didn't mean it and that this would ruin his chances to get a job and have a future. She didn't want to feel any responsibility toward screwing things up for him. Brook thought she was crazy and two weeks later when he threatened to break into her apartment in Sussex if she didn't let him in to see her she knew she needed the order of protection. Then he disappeared.

She moved to Mercy when the house came up for sale this last summer. Her cousin Everly knew his friend Greg and they were starting to date. It was how Faith found out that Andrew cheated on her with some woman he met when he got fired. He was out all night drinking and having sex with some woman and then showed up at her place days later taking out his anger on her for breaking up with him and not accepting his mistakes. It had been a nightmare.

She suddenly felt very alone and very scared. She even stopped talking to Everly because she always asked what Faith would do if Andrew came back to make things up to her. She asked if Faith was going out on dates or sleeping with anyone. She had a feeling her cousin was more interested in pleasing Greg, who controlled her, than she cared about Faith's safety.

She hurried to the front door and rechecked the locks. She then checked the windows and then the bedroom. She started to pace again, wondering what she should do. She thought about Rocky and his brothers and about Andrew's threats. Would he hurt them? Try something because she liked them? What was she going to do?

* * * *

Conan slid his hand along Brook's ass as she climbed up off of him to look at her cell phone.

"Just leave it. It's Sunday," Kinchley barked.

She stood up and Kernan walked out of the bathroom, his hair all wet from his shower. She eyed him over, feeling ready to make love to her men again. As she looked at her cell phone she saw the numerous missed calls from Faith and then the text messages. *"CALL ME AS SOON AS YOU GET THIS PLEASE."*

"Who is it?"

"Faith. She tried calling me several times last night and then just now. Plus text messages, too." She pulled on one of Kernan's shirts and then brought the phone to her ear.

"Is she that panicked over Rocky, Paulie and Hendrick hitting on her?" Kinchley asked, now getting up out of bed. She shrugged her shoulders but her gut clenched with concern. The phone rang one time and then Faith answered.

"Oh God, I'm so sorry, Brook. I'm sure you were with the guys and all but I'm scared and panicked and I don't know what to do."

"About Rocky and the guys?"

"That and well, last night when I got home there were flowers here."

"Wow, that was fast."

"No, not from them, from Andrew."

"What?" She raised her voice.

"Purple roses and a card, too."

"What did the card say?"

As she told her, Brook got angry. "That son of a bitch. Why now? Why would he start bothering you and send you flowers now?"

"I don't know. I didn't sleep at all last night. I was afraid he could come here or something. I don't know. I mean I don't think he would. I think he really wants me to forgive him."

"Don't do that. He can't be trusted."

"I don't want any trouble, especially not now. Everything was going so well. I can't believe this. I don't know what to do."

"Do nothing. Just wait and see if he contacts you again. I'll help you. Just go on with your life and with your plans."

"Oh God, Brook, I can't go out with Rocky, Paulie, and Hendrick. They want to teach me self-defense. Hendrick is picking me up in an hour."

"Don't be silly, of course you can go. You're going to have to let them know about Andrew anyway."

"No. No, I can't, and I don't think going out with them and letting this thing get complicated is smart."

"Why not, when you like them so much?"

She was silent.

"Wait a minute. You mean because of Andrew's threats to you, against any man you were to date or sleep with?" Brook said and she knew she grabbed the attention of her three men. She swallowed hard.

"He does not have control over you, Faith. I was there that night."

"Exactly, and what if he's worse. What if he only wants forgiveness and to move on?"

"No. You can't think that way. You're too sweet and forgiving. He knows that and he will prey on that innocence. You call me right away if you hear from him. I think you need to continue living your life, Faith. Don't let him have that invisible hold on you. He doesn't own you and he never did."

"I know that, but he scares me so much."

"I know he does, sweetie. You have every right to fear him, but that's what he'll count on to break you down and to make you question those who will really protect you. Please make sure you don't fall for his lies. Go out with Hendrick and them. Take your time with them. There's no need to rush into anything."

"It's so different with them, Brook. I like them a lot. I don't mind their pace, their commanding ways. It's different when they bark orders or just take control. I don't feel like a victim, I feel…desirable."

"I know what you mean, and that's wonderful, so don't push them away. Talk to them."

"No. I won't tell them about Andrew and about what happened."

"You should."

"It's embarrassing."

"There's nothing to be embarrassed about. You were completely innocent. He took advantage of that and he lost his shit and beat you up. You were in the hospital and thank God it was the summertime or you would have missed work or maybe been forced to go to school and let those kids see the bruises. I was there, Faith, and I know that fear you had, that you still have."

"What if I'm wrong? What if Rocky, Hendrick, or Paulie could lose their tempers and strike? I don't think I can do this. Not with men so big and capable as them."

"They won't hurt you. My men know them well. Don't go back into hiding and let Andrew have this control. Get ready for your date. Put those flowers in the trash and remain aware of your surroundings at all times. If he contacts you, call me."

"Okay, Brook. Thanks so much."

"Anytime."

Brook exhaled as Conan hugged her from behind. She leaned back against him and covered his hands with hers.

"Is she in danger?" he asked.

"I sure as hell hope not."

"What is going on? Who is this Andrew?" Kernan asked her. She faced him and Kinchley and Conan released his hold on her.

"It's a long story."

"So start talking," Kinchley said, arms crossed and looking pissed off.

She exhaled and explained all about Faith and Andrew.

"Holy shit, what a piece of crap," Kernan said.

"He completely manipulated her. She hadn't expected him to number one cheat on her, and secondly lose his job, flip out and then attack her. He could have done worse," Brook said.

"He didn't rape her though, right?" Conan asked.

"Thank God, no. They were dating for a few months, and things were getting more serious when this happened. You have to understand that Faith is very timid and shy to begin with. She doesn't see how beautiful she is and that isn't her focus in life. She loves being a teacher and taking care of the kids. She volunteers her time and she's truly a good person, but unfortunately that big heart had her falling for Andrew's control and lies. I think that's why she hasn't dated anyone since him and why she is freaking out over Rocky, Paulie, and Hendrick now."

"That's understandable. They are good men though. A lot older than her, so it could cause some issues. Rocky doesn't ever take any women seriously, but he acted different around Faith," Kernan added.

"She won't tell them about Andrew," Brook said and they all had scowls on their faces.

"She needs to, and especially if this guy starts stalking her or making threats," Kinchley stated.

"He warned her to not ever date any other man or he would kill them. It's been a year or more now, but she took that threat seriously, I guess, and she doesn't want to put Rocky and them into some sort of troubling situation because of her bad decision a year ago."

"That's insane. She'll need their protection. She's a petite little thing and her shyness and timidness is also from the aggressive behavior of her ex and his abuse of her. She has to tell the men," Conan said to her.

"I can't force her to."

"Well, maybe we could give them the heads up. Maybe let them know to go slow and that she was hurt before and leave it at that," Kernan suggested.

"You seriously think that will work with men like Rocky, Hendrick, and Paulie? I know them from SWAT, they will want answers. Leave it alone for now and if things progress then she will have to tell them, or I will then."

"I don't like it. It has the makings for a disaster," Conan said.

"We'll see, and in the meantime I'm going to try and find out exactly where Andrew is."

"Then what?" Kinchley asked.

"All depends on his intentions with Faith and whether or not he needs a little reminder about staying clear of her or else."

Conan pulled her into his arms. "Not alone, you aren't."

"Like I haven't had to put the pressure on someone alone before?" she asked and ran her palms up and down his chest. He lifted her up by her ass cheeks and she straddled his waist.

"Those days are over, women. We're a team now and we handle things together."

She held his gaze and a serious expression.

"Thank you, Conan. I love you guys, and I'm concerned for Faith. I hope this doesn't turn into a nightmare situation."

"If it does then we all have her back and will protect her from this guy, but guaranteed, Rocky, Hendrick, and Paulie beat us all to it," Kinchley said and she nodded and then kissed Conan as he backstepped to the bed, fell back and rocked his hips up against her, indicating he was ready to make love again. She was game definitely. She loved her men and they loved her. That's what she wanted for Faith.

* * * *

Hendrick pulled into Faith's driveway a few minutes early. As he got out and a light breeze began to blow, the cover came off of her garbage pail that was by the side of the house. He saw her front door open and he gave a wave.

"The cover came off your garbage pail. I'll just grab it and put it back on."

Her eyes widened and she pushed the storm door open as he headed to the garbage. His eyes landed on a gorgeous extra large bouquet of purple roses. He never saw anything like them before, and it appeared they were stuffed into the pail.

"I can get that," she said and reached for the cover he had picked up.

"These look brand new. They were sent to you?" he asked her, eyeing her over and he could tell she looked nervous and, well, guilty. He wasn't a patient man at all as he put the lid back on and took in the sight of her. She wore a pair of loose-fitting joggers, a V-neck T-shirt in blue and a pair of sneakers.

"Let me just grab my bag," she said and he followed her into her house, definitely wanting to know about the flowers. As he entered her front door and took in the sight of her place, he inhaled. It smelled like her and it was neat and clean. Immaculate, actually, and like no one lived there. Like it was for show. She smoothed her hands along her pants.

"Is this good to wear for training? I wasn't sure. Some places like you wearing those martial arts pants."

"This will be nice and casual. You want to be comfortable, especially when we start rolling around on the mats," he said, looking over her body and imagining wrapping her up with one arm and slinging her over his shoulder before he lowered her to the mats and pressed between her open legs. She would be begging for mercy as he tickled her before he kissed her breathless. His dick immediately hardened as she stared at him.

"Bathing suit, too?" he said.

"I'm wearing it," she told him and then grabbed her bag and the towel.

"This is a really nice place you have. It's so neat."

"That's easy to do when you live alone," she told him as they headed outside and she locked her front door. He opened the passenger side of the truck for her and she grabbed on to the handle and hoisted herself up. It gave him a nice view of her ass and the opportunity to grab her hips and help her up. She gasped and he gave her a stern expression. He closed the door and got inside.

"This truck is huge," she said, appearing small and feminine in the passenger seat.

"It's perfect for me and for my brothers. We need the room." She swallowed hard.

"So, back to the flowers. Who were they from?" he asked as he revved the diesel engine and headed down her block and to the main roadway.

"They were sent to me by mistake," she said and looked out the window.

She was lying and he got a bad feeling in his gut. As they got to the traffic light he stopped the truck, placed his hand on her crossed legs and she looked at him with that surprised, shy expression he was getting used to. "Don't ever lie to me or my brothers. That's one thing we will never accept from anyone. Man or woman," he said firmly and then the light turned green, her eyes widened and he started to drive again. He kept his hand on her thigh, wished she weren't wearing pants but instead shorts so he could feel her smooth skin beneath the palms of his hands.

"I don't want to be lied to either. Just so you know." He glanced at her and then back to the road.

"It's personal and today you're just teaching me some self-defense," she whispered.

He squeezed her thigh, making her move closer to him. She complied and scooted across the seat. "It's more than that and you know it." He made the turn onto the side road leading up to their house.

"A first date then?" she asked.

"Darling, I haven't been on a date since I was in middle school." He pulled the truck along the side of the garage where the dojo was.

"Well, I'm old fashioned, I guess, or maybe not like women you're used to," she said to him.

He parked the truck, turned off the engine and looked at her. He had one arm resting on the steering wheel as he turned toward her and the other hand smoothed between her legs as he held her gaze. "Does that mean I won't be getting a taste of your sweet cream today, Miss Old Fashioned?"

Her cheeks went flush, and she looked panicked and adorable as he laughed then cupped her cheek and kissed her. He wanted more. Desired her so much as he picked her up—she was light as a feather—and deposited her onto his lap. He dipped her slightly, making her gasp, and then he kissed her again. She kissed him back, ran her hand up into his hair and then to his shoulder. When he slid his palm under her T-shirt he hit material and he pulled from her mouth.

"What's this?" he asked, and pushed the top up a little higher.

"My bathing suit," she said as if he were crazy.

She didn't wear a bikini? She wasn't going to show off her sexy skin and tight abs and holy shit, she was really shy. It confused the fuck out of him and he stared at her like she was so strange, then tears filled her eyes.

"I told you guys this wouldn't work out. That you're used to different women than who I am." She tried getting up but he gripped her wrists and held her hands against his chest. She looked shocked. Hell, he was shocked by what he was feeling and also by how her wrists fit into one hand.

"You really are shy." She swallowed hard.

He stared at her and had a thousand questions. He wanted to interrogate her and know the truth. Was she for real, but out of all the questions he should ask right now he asked her what was on his mind. "Who sent you the damn flowers, and is he competition?"

Tears filled her eyes and she shook her head. "Someone asking for forgiveness."

"For what?"

She was quiet a few seconds. "For hurting me?" He squinted, felt his chest tighten.

"Hurting you how and when?"

She shook her head. "I don't want to ruin this day. I came here in hopes of you and your brothers being honest and good men like Brook swore you are. I can't tell you much more. Being here is a huge enough step."

He licked his lower lip and every instinct told him there was danger in her past, in this situation, but he couldn't, he wouldn't push right now. Another day, and if Brook was aware then so were Conan, Kinchley, and Kernan and he could find out from them if Faith refused to confide in him.

"Okay for now, but when you're ready I expect more information, understand?" he asked and she nodded.

"Now, how about we get started in the dojo?" She lifted up and he stopped her.

"A kiss first," he teased her and she lifted closer as she cupped his cheek so gently and pressed her lips to his. That was it for him. He already cared way too much for a fling or first date, and more than he ever cared for a woman he wanted to fuck. He was in deep trouble here, and so were his brothers.

* * * *

Paulie walked into the dojo and watched Hendrick as he taught Faith a few moves on the punching bag. She had red fingerless gloves on her hands and he was adjusting her hips. When she went to punch the bag her large breasts bounced and she looked adorable. Especially standing there barefoot with Hendrick towering over her. "Put more hip into it. Make that punch come from way back here and then throw it straight through," he said and as she came back he cleared his throat and she smiled and then swung, missed the bag and hit Hendrick.

She gasped and Hendrick shook his head, had his hands on his hips and yelled at Paulie.

"You had to interrupt just then. She almost has the right form." Hendrick grunted. Paulie slipped off his sandals he wore from the house and got onto the mat.

"Her form looks pretty good."

"No, her hips need to move better and with the momentum of her punch."

"I think her hips look fine," Paulie said, caressing her around the waist and then drawing her close to him. "Hey, beautiful," he said and stared down into her baby blue eyes. Her cheeks flushed and he pressed his lips to hers.

"I thought we were teaching her self-defense?" Rocky asked, coming into the room, too.

Paulie pulled back slowly. "You look good, sweetie. Listen to Hendrick's instructions, he knows what he's doing," he said and winked at her.

Rocky approached and looked her over. "Learn anything yet?" he asked.

"A little bit," she said shyly.

Paulie stepped aside and Rocky grabbed a handful of her T-shirt and pulled her toward him. He stared down into her eyes. "You sure are a little thing," he said then kissed her tenderly. It was short but obviously packed one hell of a punch because as he released her lips Faith's eyes remained closed.

"Back to work," Hendrick said firmly and she opened her eyes and looked at him.

"Okay. What's next?"

"Learn this first and then we move on."

"I got it," she said to him.

"Oh yeah, then show me."

She stepped back, put her gloves in front of her and then pivoted her hips as she punched the bag.

"Awesome!" Paulie said.

"That was on a bag. Now try it on a person," Hendrick told her.

"What?" she asked and Paulie could see her demeanor change.

Hendrick got into position. "I'm coming at you, what do you do?" he asked. She stepped back.

"No. Come at me with that right jab," he said to her.

"I could hurt you," she said to him and Paulie and Rocky chuckled.

"I doubt it, now try," he said.

"Do I have to? I feel more comfortable punching the bag."

"Of course you do but in real life situations you may have to hit another human being."

"I don't want to," she said and Hendrick stood up straight, scrunched his eyes at her and she swung, hitting him in the stomach. Rocky and Paulie laughed as Hendrick bent over and she apologized. "See, that's why I didn't want to do it,"

He growled and she screamed and laughed as Hendrick lifted her up over his shoulder then lowered her to the mats. He gripped her hands and placed her wrists above her head as she straddled his hips.

"You are in for it now."

"Don't you dare, Hendrick. No, no, no." She screamed and laughed as Hendrick held her wrists above her head with one hand and used the other hand to tickle her. She was screaming and laughing and then he paused. Stared down at her lips and started kissing her. Paulie looked at Rocky and no words were spoken. Faith was definitely special.

* * * *

Faith was shaking after rolling around on the mats with Hendrick and now standing by their inground swimming pool staring at their perfect bodies. The three men were covered in muscles and even had tattoos. Fierce ones with intricate black and red designs and even

American flags. Hendrick's forearms, biceps and triceps were so long, thick and muscular she felt palpitations even more so than when she was underneath him on the mats in the gym. They could crush her, heck, encase her entire body and no one would even know she was underneath one of them.

She gulped and took a sip of her bottle of water before she got enough nerve up to pull off her clothes and show her black bathing suit. Normally when she sunbathed she would wear a bikini, but any pool parties or gatherings with friends she wore this one. It was less revealing, yet raised high on her thighs, and dipped low in her back as well as the front. It had support for her large breasts, which right now were on alert and completely aware of the three sexy men watching her.

"Are you coming in?" Paulie asked, staring at her as he stood in the pool and then leaned against the side. She was so hot, and not just sweaty from the gym and the hot temperatures either. She hoped the water was cold.

"Is it cold?" she asked.

The sound of country music filtered through the air as Rocky put on the radio. It was coming from surround sound speakers where the cabana was and even in the pool. They knew she was shy and nervous as Hendrick went under the water to cool off and then Paulie did the same. Rocky started walking in by the steps and she took the opportunity to pull off her pants and the tank top, then raised her arms up to place her hair on top of her head so it wouldn't get soaked.

When she turned around Rocky smiled at her. She walked to the steps and dipped her foot in. "You look really good, sweetie. I'm glad you're here," he said to her and she smiled.

"Jump in, it feels great, then we'll start cooking up some lunch," Paulie said and she made her way into the pool, glad that it was cool enough to take away some of the heat in her body until Paulie grabbed her and dipped her in his arms.

"You are filled with surprises, sweetie," he said and looked at her lips and then at her breasts.

"Why is that?" she asked.

"You just are." He stared into her eyes. "Do you want to kiss me?" She nodded her head.

"Then stop torturing me, woman," he said, sounding breathless and Faith leaned forward and pressed her lips to his. It was erotic and sexy, being in his arms, her skin against his skin, and the feeling of being protected and cared for outweighed her fears. She lifted up and ran her fingers through his hair then felt the second set of hands on her. She was now cradled between Paulie and Rocky.

Lips pressed against her skin on her shoulder and then toward her neck. Rocky suckled hard against a sensitive spot as Paulie continued to deepen the kiss. She felt the water move, then her body shift, hands lifted her from under the water and then Rocky used his teeth to lower the strap of her bathing suit. She pulled from Paulie's lips. Their hold tightened.

"Easy, doll," Rocky said to her and she was breathing heavily.

"We feel it, too. Let us explore a little. We won't go far," he added and leaned down to lick along her breast, pouring from the top.

"We shouldn't. It's too much."

"Best way to get to know one another is to explore these feelings, don't you think?" Paulie asked her and stroked her jaw with his finger. She stared up into his dark blue eyes and he nodded.

"Trust us, Faith. We're good men. We won't take advantage of you. You say stop and we stop."

She wanted to feel more, and she didn't want to come off like some prude or something. She nodded her head.

"Words," Hendrick said firmly. She stared at him.

"Okay," she whispered.

"Good. Now, do you like when Paulie kisses you and touches you?" Rocky asked.

"Yes," she said and Paulie stroked her jaw and then down her throat to her breast.

"How about when I touch you at the same time."

"I like it."

"Thank God," Hendrick whispered and they chuckled. She wondered if she was making them feel as nervous as they made her feel.

Rocky began to lower the strap to her top on one side as he kissed along her neck and shoulder. "Feel good?" he whispered and then kissed and suckled a little more firmly.

"Yes," she said in a sigh, then Paulie touched his lips to hers and she kissed him. Hendrick slid his palms up her thighs under the water and then Rocky kissed her skin lower and lower until a breast emerged and he suckled her nipple. She moaned into Paulie's mouth and Rocky suckled harder. Then fingers slid along her thighs and then Paulie shifted and Hendrick slid her strap down on the other side and his mouth explored her other breast. They were holding her up between them as each man suckled on a part of her. She was shocked and so incredibly aroused when she started moving her hips and then gasped and came.

Paulie pulled from her lips. "Holy shit, baby."

Fuck," Hendrick said and slid his palms to her ass and squeezed her. He lifted her higher and then lowered his mouth to her pussy right over her bathing suit, shocking her.

"Hendrick!" she exclaimed and wiggled and pushed free from them.

"Whoa, slow down," Rocky said to her and pulled her into his arms as she fixed her top.

"You were coming in our arms. Why are you stopping this?" Hendrick demanded.

"Hendrick, you're scaring her. She was shaking," Rocky said to him in warning.

"Why did you stop me, us?" he demanded to know.

"It's too much. I shouldn't have let you do that."

"No, you should have because it was perfect," Paulie said as he reached out and stroked her cheek.

"You're aroused and turned on by us just as we are by you, why did you stop it from continuing?" Hendrick pushed.

"This isn't even a first date. I hardly know you."

"You feel the attraction. You like our touch and you want more. Your body doesn't lie, Faith. Why stop it?" he asked firmly.

"It's too much," she said and started to walk from the pool.

Hendrick got in front of her. "Does this have to do with the flowers?" he asked her, shocking her. She opened her mouth to say something and nothing came out.

"What flowers?" Rocky asked.

"Someone sent her purple roses and they were in her garbage. It was new and a big arrangement. She lied to me earlier and said they were sent to her by mistake." He raised his voice.

"What? Are you seeing someone else? Were they from another guy?" Paulie asked.

"Stop this. Why are you doing this, Hendrick? Can't you just leave it alone?"

"No, it's why you're stopping us from exploring these feelings and I want to know who the dick is," he demanded.

"That isn't why I stopped it. It's too much. I'm not as experienced as you guys are. You're obviously used to having your way with women who come here as you seduce them into bed. That isn't me." She started toward the stairs and Hendrick grabbed her hand and pulled her into his arms.

"Don't you dare do that. Don't compare yourself to other women and women like that who are easy. We like spending time with you and we want you, plain and simple. That's the truth."

She parted her lips and then she felt the tears in her eyes. She had to be honest. She was ruining this time with them. She didn't want that. She wouldn't let Andrew ruin it either.

She cupped Hendrick's cheeks as Rocky and Paulie approached.

"I sort of lied, because I didn't want to show my distress or let those flowers ruin this first date with you guys."

"So they were from a guy?" Hendrick asked.

"It was a mistake because he has no right to send them."

"Who the fuck is he?" Rocky demanded to know.

She reached out to him. "Please calm down. There's no need to be jealous or angry. I'm sure you have secrets, or relationships from the past you never want to revisit," she said to him.

"This guy hurt you or something?" Paulie asked her. She nodded her head. Hendrick looked pissed.

"Please, Hendrick, I don't handle aggression and confrontations well. I like calmness, serenity, not chaos and being upset."

"Well, it's kind of what I feel, not knowing exactly why this guy, an ex, I assume, sent you such an elaborate bouquet of purple roses."

"To get under my skin. To see if he can control me still."

"Control you?" Rocky asked her. Tears filled her eyes. She couldn't stop them.

"This isn't over, is it?" Hendrick asked.

"I believed it to be over. I haven't heard from him in over a year. It was a shock to come home from the event yesterday and find a delivery guy there waiting."

She figured she could give them some information but not everything. She didn't need them feeling sorry for her or worse, feeling annoyed with her for allowing a man to control her then beat her in anger.

"I'd rather not talk about this and ruin the day," she said to them.

"Oh no, we are definitely talking about this, sweetie, and remember, no lies to us, ever," Hendrick said and then they made their way out of the pool.

* * * *

Hendrick couldn't help the sensations he had. His gut clenched and his gut was never wrong. Could this guy, this situation have something to do with Faith's shyness?

They grabbed some towels and she wrapped herself up in one and then took a seat in the sun. She stared at them as they gathered around her.

"I don't want to do this," she whispered. Rocky reached over and caressed her knee.

"We just have a few questions. To ensure that you're okay. This guy, is he a problem? Someone who might try and come back into your life?" Rocky asked her and Hendrick watched her body language, and the way her eyes held his brother's gaze.

"I hope not. Things ended badly. He wasn't right for me. I met him only a month or so after moving to Sussex."

"You lived in Sussex?" Paulie asked. She looked away and barely smiled, an indicator that she was trying to hide her true emotions.

"There wasn't anything in Mercy at the time that fit my budget. I moved here from New Jersey on a whim, really. I took a chance, applied for the teaching job and was shocked that I got it. I hadn't quite planned it out thoroughly so I took whatever I could grab quickly. I didn't want to worry about wasting time finding the right place while I needed to get things ready for the school year. There were a lot of changes going on. I was a little vulnerable at the time."

"What do you mean changes?" Paulie asked.

"Vulnerable why? Because you moved out here alone?" Hendrick asked.

She leaned back, let the towel fall from her body and she crossed her legs. She was classy and sexy. She placed her hands on her lap and looked at them as she spoke.

"My family isn't really close. My brother is in the military and he kept taking tour after tour and was stationed overseas. He lives in Germany and is some higher up or something. I barely talk to him. My parents retired and have been traveling and enjoying life. I was sitting around wanting a family, a support network and when it came to getting offered this job there was no one to talk to and process the decision with. I figured they all did their own thing, ya know, so why shouldn't I do mine? It wasn't like they call or ask how I am."

"That's not fair, baby. How long have you been taking care of yourself?" Rocky asked and reached over to caress her cheek. She chuckled.

"A long time, but I got up the nerve to leave New Jersey. To worry about me, my life and what I wanted. My family wasn't really a family anymore so I took the chance."

"That took a lot of guts," Hendrick said and he couldn't help but to think about his parents and especially his father. The man was abusive in so many ways. A drunk, a batterer, and someone he and his brothers learned to hate. Especially as their mother suffered and wouldn't leave him. When it came to cases like that with work, it was always so hard to handle. He cleared his mind and focused on Faith. It didn't sound like her parents were abusive, it sounded like they gave up on being there and became self-centered.

"How did you handle the move here alone and meeting people like Brook, Emma, and Casey?" Paulie asked.

She smiled and then talked about her boss, the principal, and how she helped her find a place and then attend a fundraising event of Kai's where she met Brook, Casey, and Emma.

"We hit it off and they were so nice. I got to know Corporal's, but I barely went there." She looked away.

"Why is that?" Paulie asked.

She smiled and then worried her bottom lip. Something she did when she was nervous, and even at a loss for words. She took a deep breath and exhaled.

"Pretty sure you noticed it, but I'm very shy. It's just my nature to hold back and to watch and listen. I put so much into my job that by the time the weekend comes, I'm tired and just want to relax, so I wind up doing that alone. My friends call and call and finally I give in and go out with them, but crowds, bars, they make me feel uncomfortable."

"Is that because of all the guys that hit on you?" Rocky asked, eyeing her over. Hendrick felt that instant jealous feeling. She was a knockout.

"Guys don't hit on me. Not the right ones, anyway. I think it's the glasses," she said and lowered her eyes. Paulie reached over and cupped her chin, tilted it up toward him.

"You look fucking sexy as damn hell with your glasses, and your sophisticated hairstyle. You give off a radiance of class, sweetness and sexy all combined. That's what makes you so damn attractive," he told her then pressed his lips to hers. When he eased back she just stared at him.

"I still want to know about this guy and the purple roses," Hendrick interrupted. She looked at him as Paulie released her chin and she looked nervous.

"I met Andrew shortly after meeting the ladies. I thought he was perfect. Handsome, mature, a soldier like my friends hung out with, but as time went on things changed."

"He's a soldier? Does he live around here?" Rocky asked.

"I don't think so. I don't know where he lives. I have a cousin, Everly. She lives outside of Mercy, and even though she is blood, I'm not really close to her. She started to see a friend of Andrew's and so we double dated several times, but Everly isn't really the commitment type. Like I said earlier, hanging out, doing the bar scene isn't my thing."

"About Andrew, what happened."

She stared at him.

"Bottom line? He cheated on me."

"What?" Rocky asked.

She exhaled, looked away and then stared at her hands, wringing her fingers together.

"I thought he was great, and fit into my life. He was working hard for some construction company and then there were problems. He wanted a higher position and was turned down. He was angry about that and I guess him and Greg were out drinking and Everly and her friends caught him with another woman. He admitted to having sex with her."

"What an asshole," Paulie said and caressed her hair.

She looked at him. "He was angry when I broke things off. He blamed me, and the fact that we dated for months and I wouldn't sleep with him."

"What?" Hendrick asked.

She looked at him and then she stood up. She started to fold the towel as she spoke, like she needed to do something to keep busy and not really face what she was talking about. It was obvious the dick hurt her.

"It wasn't right of him to say the things he did or to do the things he did. This is my body and I decide if and when I want to give it to a man. I'm just so glad I didn't have sex with him. God, what am I doing? I shouldn't be having this conversation with you."

Hendrick pulled her between his legs where he sat on the chair. "No, you should be. We want you to feel comfortable talking to us. What you've explained helps us to understand your shyness and your reservations. We aren't like this guy though. We want you to know that."

She reached up and caressed his cheek. "I feel that you aren't but my mind is fighting my heart right now. I haven't dated anyone since Andrew because I felt like I was a bad judge of character. I mean he seemed perfect." She caressed his cheek and he caressed her ass and her back.

"Then when I was getting closer to giving in to his demands and about to have sex with him, he cheated."

"Aw, baby," Rocky said, standing up and placing his hands on her shoulders. They towered over her. She was so feminine and sweet and Hendrick wanted to tear this dick apart and then he thought about the flowers.

"He sent you those roses. You know he's trying to get back into your life?"

"I won't let him. He's made me waste so much time as is. I've been afraid to go out, to meet anyone else out of the fears of getting hurt and being used. This is such a big risk, coming here, letting you do what you did to me in the pool. God, it's crazy," she said and covered her face with her hands.

"Not crazy, but perfect. That's the difference. You felt comfortable and you let your guard down and enjoyed it," Rocky told her and kissed her bare shoulder.

"We definitely enjoyed it, too," Paulie said and winked at her as she uncovered her face. She was flushed as Hendrick massaged her ass and then trailed his thumbs under the elastic of her bathing suit over her upper thighs and groin. Her lips parted.

"Trust us to bring you pleasure. To make you feel beautiful and perfect like you are," he said to her and leaned forward to kiss her belly against the one-piece bathing suit she wore. He felt her fingers running through his hair and then he heard her moan as Paulie cupped her cheeks and kissed her.

Rocky pulled her arms behind her as he suckled against her neck and as Hendrick looked up, Rocky slid the straps to her bathing suit down and her breasts emerged, so big, full and with erect nipples. She moaned louder and he licked the tip, swirled his tongue around the areola while he maneuvered his hands under her bathing suit elastic.

"So responsive and sexy. You're a goddess, Faith. Such a sexy body, full large breasts, a sexy, round ass and—"

She jerked forward and Hendrick knew his brother Rocky was stroking her cunt from behind. She bent forward slightly as Hendrick suckled harder and Paulie devoured her moans.

"That's it. So wet. Fuck, you're coming like a faucet. Your body knows, baby. Knows that we're real men who will protect you, take care of you and bring you nothing but pleasure. Holy fuck. Ride my fingers, Faith. Come on, girl, rock those hips and show me how good it feels," he said and she pulled from Paulie's mouth and cried out her release. Her head was against Hendrick's shoulder as Rocky continued to thrust his fingers into her cunt from behind.

Paulie bent down and latched on to her other breast. "Paulie!" she exclaimed and Hendrick followed his lead and suckled her breast. She lifted up.

"I need more," Rocky grunted out. He released her arms and she grabbed on to Hendrick.

"Spread those thighs now," Rocky ordered and Hendrick felt her shaking.

"Oh God, this isn't happening. Oh God I can't, I—"

Smack.

"Oh!"

"Do it, baby. Do it because this feels so good, so right and you are loving three men wanting you, wanting this body and to claim you ours. Spread those legs now, Faith. That's an order," Rocky commanded and she moaned again, lowered her head and spread her thighs. Rocky lowered down to his knees, pushed aside her bathing suit and sucked against her clit and pussy. She was bent totally over Hendrick's shoulder, and Hendrick grabbed on to her ass cheek. He squeezed and massaged it as his brother held the bathing suit to the side and sucked and moaned against her cunt.

"That's it, baby. Give it to him. Good girls get rewarded," Paulie said as he brought her hand to his cock and she gasped, cried out and came.

Rocky fixed her bathing suit and Hendrick pulled her into his arms and carried her into the cabana. There was a large round lounging couch and he lowered her to it. He pressed between her legs and stared into her flushed cheeks, her glistening eyes and just stared at her. "You look gorgeous." He pressed his lips to her nose, to her cheeks and then her lips.

"I can't believe I let you guys do that to me," she said as Rocky stood by the couch and Paulie slid up and next to her. He ran his palm up her thigh to her breast and cupped it then thumbed her nipple.

"I want a taste, too," he said and she widened her eyes.

"I think maybe we should slow down."

"I think maybe you need to learn to share equally," Paulie said and then slid down her strap on one side and started to feast on her breast. She moaned and tilted her hips upward. Hendrick pushed down the other strap, exposing both breasts fully.

"God damn, she is fit for a king," Rocky said.

"Fit for three kings," Hendrick said and then began to feast on her breast. She tried lifting her hands up but both men gripped them. Hendrick released her breast.

"Let us pleasure you, baby."

"I don't want to go too far. This is so much already," she said in a panic.

"Only as far as you want."

"My brothers need to taste that sweet, delicious cream. Let them, Faith, and I promise you won't regret it," Rocky said. He stood at the edge of the lounging couch, watching them. Hendrick and Paulie began to push her bathing suit off of her.

"Oh God, I'll be naked."

"You wore a one piece. Next time wear a bikini," Rocky said to her and she gasped as Paulie and Hendrick removed her bathing suit and Paulie slid over her, spread her thighs and went right to her cunt.

"Paulie!" she cried out and reached for his head but then Rocky approached and gripped her hands and wrists and lifted them above her. Her torso lifted up.

"Oh God, please. Please don't hurt me," she said. Hendrick was shocked and so was Rocky but Rocky quickly lowered his mouth to hers. He whispered against her lips. "Never would we ever, ever hurt you, Faith. We will bring you pleasure. Relax and let go. We got you," he said and pressed his lips to hers.

Faith thrust upward and Paulie moaned against her cunt. He pulled back. "She's coming like a faucet," he said, lips wet and eyes wide and looking fierce.

"My turn," Hendrick stated firmly and he took Paulie's position and Paulie moved onto his side and cupped her breast. "You taste so good, Faith. So fucking delicious," he said and Rocky released her lips and lowered his mouth to her other breast.

"Oh God, please. Please, Hendrick, I feel something. What is that? Oh God," she cried out and rocked her hips. Hendrick lowered to his chest, lifted her thighs over his shoulders and then licked her from cunt to anus. Back and forth he stimulated her asshole and her cunt, plunging his tongue into her cunt and then sliding fingers into both holes.

"Oh!" she cried out and he felt her explode.

"Holy shit, bro, you got her there," Paulie said.

"Keep it going. Break her down. Make our woman see how perfect she is, and that she belongs to us," Rocky said and she moaned louder and then cried out again and again. Hendrick was relentless with his strokes of fingers then tongue and then she came one more time and he felt about ready to explode. He wanted nothing more than to sink his cock into every hole. To claim her right now and never let her out of his sight, but he remembered her words. She dated that dick for months and didn't sleep with him. She was with them for an hour and here she was naked and pliant in their arms, letting them pleasure her. The walls would go soon enough. This would have to do for now.

* * * *

Faith was shocked at the turn of events. She felt sedated, content as the men kissed her everywhere their mouths could touch. They even washed her up and then covered her with a light towel. She held it against her chest and exhaled as Rocky caressed her body against his.

"You are so very beautiful. Especially when you're coming," he whispered to her and kissed her shoulder and neck.

"I can't believe I just let the three of you do that to me."

"You know it feels right. That there won't be anything to fear with the three of us wanting you, and being your men."

"What?" she asked and turned to look at him. Hendrick sat in the chair and watched her. Paulie sat in another chair and watched her, as well.

"We want you to be our woman. We want to make you ours and we want to be yours. Like the relationships Brook, Casey, and Emma have with their men," Rocky told her as he stroked her jaw.

She was instantly scared. She didn't know what to expect with Andrew contacting her. She didn't know his state of mind. She feared he could try to go after these men. How embarrassing would that be?

"Don't you want that, too?" he asked her.

"I do, but I'm so scared to take a chance."

He smiled softly and stroked her cheek.

"We'll go nice and slow. Take our time and get to know one another. We'll make plans, set dates for things so you feel comfortable."

She held his gaze and knew in her heart, in her gut that he was being sincere. "I believe you. But what we did today definitely didn't fall under going slow."

They chuckled.

"You were game and we were definitely game, too. It's bound to happen again and again. Nothing wrong with doing a little exploring," Paulie said to her.

She could see Paulie's shorts were tented out in front, and so were Hendrick's. Could she reciprocate and make them not push for sex since she wasn't ready? Well, maybe she was ready. Nothing felt so perfect as it did when she was with them and their mouths and hands were on her. But then it was new and anything could happen.

She pressed her hands to Rocky's chest. His eyes squinted at her.

"I'm not ready to have sex with you guys. I waited a long time with—"

"Shhh, don't say his fucking name," Rocky snapped at her and she was both intimidated and aroused by his jealousy.

"I want to taste you, too," she said, voice cracking.

"Holy fuck," Paulie whispered.

Rocky lifted his hand to her cheek and gripped her chin.

"Only if you want to, not because you think you have to in order to please me, to please us."

She was shocked and it brought tears to her eyes.

"I'm not very experienced, Rocky, but for some reason, you, Paulie and Hendrick make me want to explore things, and try things I was fearful of trying."

"Never be afraid with us. Take your time, baby. We're all yours."

She lifted up, and felt the towel fall from her body, heard the intakes of breath from behind her as Paulie and Hendrick got the perfect view of her naked body. She climbed up onto Rocky. He was so big, thick and wide. She felt feminine, sexy and like she could be some kind of seductress as he slid his palm to her ass while she pressed her lips to his. His fingers stroked the crack and wild thoughts went through her head. A ménage relationship meant every hole would be claimed. Her friends carried on about the sex, about the connections they felt to their men and she wanted that, too. She yearned to be loved, to be protected and actually cared about. She needed to slow her mind down. She was the one who needed slow and not fast. This had to mean something.

She undid his shorts and pushed them down with his help. She then kissed along his pectoral muscles, inhaled his cologne and absorbed the feel of his fingers against her asshole and then one finger stroked into her cunt. She paused, moaned and tilted her head up.

"Beautiful," Rocky whispered and she refocused and slid her tongue along his skin straight to his cock.

"Fuck, baby, yeah, just like that. Oh God, Faith," Rocky moaned and lifted his hips. She had a hard time sucking in his thick, hard cock. He was super big and thick but she suddenly wanted to please him.

Wanted to make him wild with desire for her and see her as a seductress, not a weak, timid woman.

She lowered her head up and down, then moaned loudly when she felt the finger slide into her cunt from behind. A hand was splayed over her ass and Hendrick used his fingers as if they were a cock and he thrust them into her pussy.

"So fucking wet and tight. You are a goddess, woman," Hendrick chanted. The couch dipped and Paulie was there, naked, cock in hand. She moaned as she continued to suck up and down on Rocky's cock.

"I'm next, woman," Paulie said and he eased a hand up to her ass. Hendrick slid her cream over her asshole and then Paulie pressed a finger into her ass. A gush of cream shot from her cunt.

"Holy fuck, that is hot. She's coming all over our fingers. She liked being filled with our fingers, Rocky. Her ass is so tight."

"So is her cunt," Hendrick said and she moaned and rocked her hips as Rocky grunted and came. She swallowed him as quickly as she could but her body was overwhelmed with sensations.

"My turn." Paulie's fingers slid from her ass and she grunted.

"Oh God."

"Don't worry, Rocky will take his place fingering that ass. You get that mouth on Paulie's cock," Hendrick commanded.

She moaned and then Paulie was there, sliding under her and he brought his cock to her mouth. "Come on, baby, take me into that wet mouth. I want to feel you claim my cock. Do it," he ordered and she felt her pussy clench.

"She loves being ordered around. Holy fuck, she is going to be an incredible lover. Fuck," Hendrick said and then lowered his mouth to her pussy. She felt it and then she felt Rocky's fingers slide into her asshole. It was too much as she grunted but then Paulie pushed his cock between her lips. She wanted to please him, too. To give them this because she wasn't ready for sex yet. She couldn't be that intimate with them, yet this felt very intimate. Very naughty, too.

"Don't lose focus and panic. Suck my cock, woman. Come on now. You can handle it. I know we're big men but you were made for us. Come on, baby, yes, just like that. Holy hell. Fuck, Fuck," Paulie carried on and thrust his hips upward. She grabbed on to his hips and sucked and bobbed her head up and down.

"I'm there. Holy shit." Paulie grunted and came. She swallowed his essence, absorbed his scent and the firmness of his fingers in her hair as she sucked and then released his cock as it softened. He pulled her closer and kissed her. She felt the fingers leave her ass and cunt and then Paulie rolled her to her side.

"I can't wait to sink my cock into your pussy and claim you my woman. I can't fucking wait," he said and kissed her with vigor and purpose.

Hendrick cleared his throat and Paulie released her lips.

"Hendrick needs you next," he said and stroked her jaw. She felt feminine, petite and her jaw ached a little but she was determined to please them. As he lifted up she caught sight of Hendrick, naked, stroking a thick, long cock and she felt her body shaking.

"No fears. You got this," he said to her. Hendrick leaned over and stroked her nipple. He slid over her body between her legs and his cock hit her overly-sensitive pussy. She moaned.

He cupped her cheeks as he leaned above her, partially crushing her. "I can claim you right now. We can make it official today. Just say yes and I'll slide my cock right into your sweet cunt and claim you, woman. I fucking want you."

"I can't. It's too soon. It's—"

"Okay, but know we want to." He rolled to his back and she kissed his mouth. She slid her hands up his chest and then rocked her body against his thick, hard muscles. He was super big and strong. Rock solid everywhere and the tattoos aroused her but also made her nervous. What were these men capable of?

She lowered down and he ran his fingers through her hair and just as she took the tip of his cock into her mouth, Rocky moved in behind her. He rubbed his thick hard cock against her folds then down her ass. She tightened up.

"I want you to feel what you do to us. How wild you make us," he told her.

Smack. He spanked her ass and then slid a finger into her cunt. His other hand possessively held her hip and he rocked against her ass. She moaned and bobbed her head up and down on Hendrick's cock. She put all her desire into sucking him down and all she wanted into taking from him. She knew she couldn't have sex with them. It was too soon and she was fearful to take the chance. She only just met them. This was a first date of sorts and look where they were. Naked on a lounge chair in their cabana.

"Oh yeah, Faith, that feels so good. Your mouth feels incredible," Hendrick told her as he rocked his hips upward.

"She is super fucking sexy. Our little school teacher has a naughty side. Not so prim and proper," Paulie said and he slid his finger into her ass. She lost it. She moaned and felt the cream gush from her cunt and then Rocky's mouth replaced his fingers.

"I'm there, baby. Holy fuck, I'm there," Hendrick said and shot his load down her throat. She sucked and licked him clean and then Rocky slid his mouth from her cunt.

Smack.

Smack.

"Oh!" she exclaimed and Hendrick wrapped his arms around her and rolled her to her back. He pressed between her legs and stayed there over her.

"You are incredible, Faith. This has only just begun."

She hugged him back and they lay there, naked, relaxed until Hendrick decided he needed to cool down since she wasn't ready to let them make love to her today. He lifted her up and carried her into the swimming pool.

"I've never gone skinny dipping before and definitely not in the daylight."

He covered her ass with his hand and lowered her into the water with him. She straddled his hips and he was so thick and large she couldn't even get her legs around him.

"A first with us, huh? I kind of like that," Rocky said and stroked her skin. She looked at him, in all his glory, and then at Paulie. All three men were sexual gods and here she was, a tiny little virgin, doing more with them than she ever did with any man in her life. She wanted them. She knew she did, but she wouldn't have any regrets. Wouldn't make a mistake by acting too soon. No, she needed to be sure that a ménage was what she wanted. That these three incredible men were who they claimed to be and that they could care for her, protect her, love her and complete her. As they swam around and passed her to one another, taking their time kissing her skin, whispering into her ear, telling her how sexy and beautiful she was, she knew they were it. She found three perfect men to love and give her heart, soul, and virginity to, so why was trepidation filling her gut?

Andrew.

His threats, the fact he sent her flowers and was possibly trying to get back into her life was a situation she would need to deal with. She knew that Brook had her back. She knew that she felt protective of these men already, too. They didn't need to know about the violence and how Andrew assaulted her. It would show them a weakness and vulnerability she was striving to overcome this last year. As she thought about that, she thought about how special Paulie, Hendrick, and Rocky were, and how they made her feel. Around them she felt empowered, protected and like she could do anything. She nearly giggled but instead now hugged Paulie tight as they waded in the water, enjoying being together.

They were with it. They made her feel things no one else ever did. They had to be the ones for her. They just had to be. She needed to take her time and to be sure.

Her stomach rumbled. Paulie chuckled.

"I think our baby is hungry," he said and cupped her cheeks. Then he slid his palm to her breast and cupped it. He stroked the nipple.

Rocky pressed up against her bare back, sliding his palm along her ass and the crack as he kissed her shoulder.

"Lunch, then Faith for dessert." He sucked against her skin and she moaned softly, leaned back and that was when things got started all over again. Hendrick slid a finger to her cunt as Rocky leaned her back so her body was exposed to them right there in the center of the pool. Paulie suckled her breast while he held her thigh and Rocky held her back and shoulders, his palm under her ass, stimulating her asshole, and Hendrick held her other thigh and stroked her cunt.

"Let go, woman. You belong to us. No other men but us ever again. And no other women for us. We only have eyes for you, got it," Rocky told her and slid his finger into her asshole.

"Oh God, please, please Rocky!" She thrust and wiggled and came again.

"God damn, she is gorgeous, even more so when she comes." Hendrick pulled his fingers from her cunt and Paulie lifted her up into his arms and brought her deeper into the pool where only he could stand and she had to hold on. She glanced over her shoulder as he suckled her neck and squeezed her tight. She locked gazes with Hendrick and then Rocky.

"We'll get lunch started," Rocky said and gave her a wink. She turned back toward Paulie, ran her fingers through his dark brown hair and stared into his eyes.

"I love your eyes," they both said at the same time then laughed.

"Thank you for trusting us today. For letting go. I'm sure it was a lot considering what that guy did to you."

She felt guilty now. Maybe she should come clean and tell them how Andrew attacked her, and put her in the hospital. How Brook came to her aid. But then she would have to explain why she didn't press charges and how she was trying to not be an excuse of Andrew failing or losing his job. They wouldn't understand. They were fierce, righteous American soldiers and they knew right from wrong and perhaps didn't forgive easily. No, she may not ever have to tell them the truth, and she would be fine with that.

She kissed his lips and then hugged him tight. A giddy feeling filled her belly. She was naked in a pool with Paulie. She had oral sex with them, and loved every second of it. Not too bad for a virgin. *I wonder what else they can teach me, and bring out in me?*

She chuckled and then relished in the feel of Paulie's arms wrapped around her and his palm over her ass. It felt perfect, and after everything she had gone through in her life, and after so much time alone, didn't she deserve this kind of perfect?

Chapter 5

"Are you sure this isn't a problem, Rocky? I know it's last minute and all but I'm afraid I won't make it in time to pick up Brianna. I might even get there at the same time you do or a few minutes later. I already called the principal and she knows you'll be coming. You don't even have to put the car seat in the truck or anything."

"Hailey, it's fine. You know we're here for you in anything you need."

"I know that. I appreciate it and it helps so much that the three of you are part of Brianna's life and mine."

He felt uneasy and it was because he missed his brother Keith and if he had only noticed the addiction sooner perhaps he or his brothers could have saved Keith's life. Keith was missing out on his baby girl's life.

"I'll be there, no worries."

"Thanks so much."

Rocky ended the call and looked at the clock. He had a half an hour before it was time to leave. He just needed to finish up a few more things in the house and then he would head out.

* * * *

Faith stood by the entryway to the school. She was worried about Peter. He was a little boy in her class that she and the school social worker had noticed some peculiar changes in. He was wearing loose-fitting clothing that were stained and he would flinch when he heard a loud noise or if someone bumped into him. She smiled at him as he waited for one of his parents to pick him up. He stood right next to her and she could feel his hand grip her dress. She caressed his light brown hair and he looked up at her with such sweet brown eyes. "You had a great day today, Peter. I loved the coloring you did for the project."

He smiled just slightly. When her hand slid along his shoulder and back he tightened up. It was as if he were in pain.

"Peter?" she questioned but he stepped away just as some parents arrived.

They said hello to her and waved good-bye as the monitors helped to ensure that each child went home with the right parent. She looked down at Peter as Brianna, another little girl, approached. "Miss Coleman, my daddy's—"

Some of the other kids started laughing as Brianna said something to her about her daddy coming to pick her up. At least that's what it sounded like.

"Okay, well, we'll wait right here," she told her and Brianna hugged her other leg. Faith was wearing a straight fitted burgundy dress today that reached her knees, and a pair of low heeled wedges. She waved good-bye to some of the other children as they left and noticed the big black pickup truck pull up front. She was pretty sure that was Rocky's truck. She remembered seeing it in the driveway of their home.

She instantly got excited but then Brianna yelled out, pointing at Rocky, saying, "He's here, he's here." Brianna pulled from her hand and one of the monitors welcomed Rocky. She watched in shock as Rocky bent down and Brianna jumped into his arms.

In her head she freaked. Brianna said *my daddy is coming to get me today.* She was pretty sure of it. She met her mom Hailey and didn't believe there was a father in the picture. Oh God, was that his baby but he wasn't married to Hailey? Why wouldn't he mention something major like that?

His eyes locked on to Faith. He eyed her over, smiling, but then his face changed to one of concern. She looked away and Peter grabbed her leg and hugged it tight.

"Sweetie, what's wrong?" she asked and heard the commotion by the car where two monitors were talking to a man. He was pointing at Peter.

"It's okay. Who is that, Peter?"

"My stepdad," he whispered.

Every instinct in her body went on alert. She bent down and looked at Peter." Are you scared of him?" He nodded his head.

"Has he tried to hurt you?" He nodded his head.

"That's my stepson, now let me take him home," the guy yelled.

"What's going on, Faith?" the principal asked.

Faith looked at her. "That's the stepfather. Peter is scared to go with him. You and I know how Peter has been acting. I think you need to call the police."

In her peripheral vision Faith caught sight of Brianna's mom. She was hugging Rocky hello and he hugged her back but his eyes were on Faith. She felt so hurt she wanted to cry but here she was involved with a serious situation. Perhaps a case of child abuse and she was not going to let Peter out of her sight.

"Come with me, Peter."

"What are you doing?" her principal asked.

"Getting him into the safety of the school. Get the resource officer on the walkie-talkie," Faith said as the man was heading toward them.

"Miss Coleman." Peter was sobbing.

She pulled him in front of her. "I won't let him hurt you. Listen to what I say, baby," she told him and just as they got to the door and Peter got inside where the SOR officer was coming toward them, she heard the sirens and then a hand grabbed her shoulder, pulling her back.

She reacted. Using the move that Hendrick taught her, she swung a straight jab to the guy's shoulder. It was enough of a distraction to get Peter inside and for the police to approach. She hadn't expected the man to start yelling or for him to shove her into the metal door. Her back hit the long push bar and she screamed at him as she closed the door and placed her body in front of it.

"You are not going to lay a hand on that kid. Never again!" she screamed at him. He shoved her again but then Rocky was there. He grabbed the guy by his neck and pulled him back as if he were a rag doll. The guy was on the ground and the police were arresting him.

More police arrived on scene, and when Rocky looked at her, she was scared. Scared of his strength, scared of already being in love with him and now hurt that he didn't tell her he had a child with some woman and he was involved in their lives.

"Are you okay? How is your back, Faith? I saw him shove you so hard. What the hell is going on?"

"Thanks, Rocky," one of the cops said to him, obviously knowing him.

"Miss, we'll need to talk to you." She nodded and then Hailey was there, holding on to his arm and Brianna was holding on to his leg. She looked them over and then back at him. His eyes squinted.

"Yes, officer, whatever you need," she said and walked into the building with the police right behind her as others took Peter's stepfather away in handcuffs.

* * * *

"What the fuck happened?" Hendrick asked Rocky when they arrived at the school. He and Paulie just got off work when the call came over the radio about a disturbance at the elementary school in Mercy. Hendrick called Caden and found out that Faith was involved and that there was a child abuse situation and Faith was protecting the child.

"It was crazy, but Faith wouldn't let the guy near the kid. I was here picking up Brianna for Hailey, and I think Faith totally got the wrong idea, but I haven't been able to see her or talk to her."

"She got hurt though?" Paulie asked as Caden walked out of the building with two of the police officers.

They listened while he spoke to them. "So Faith will be accompanying the child to the hospital to see his mom. They'll ride with me. Good job getting across town so quickly. We'll talk back at the department later on," Caden said to the men. Hendrick couldn't believe how concerned he was and the more he heard the details and that some child abuser was hurting a kid he thought about his own childhood, and how he and his brothers sustained some pretty intense punishments from their piece of shit father. He pushed the thoughts from his head as Caden approached.

"Thanks for assisting earlier, Rocky," Caden said to him.

"I wasn't sure what was going on, but once the guy shoved Faith into the door and she punched him, then he shoved her again, I saw red."

"Good thing you were here. She's pretty shaken up but holding strong for the little boy."

"Is Faith hurt, Caden?" Paulie asked before Hendrick could.

"I think she's bruised up pretty badly. She's refusing any medical treatment. I think she'll be in more pain later tonight. At least it's a Friday so she has the weekend off. She's going to head to the hospital with the little boy she saved. His mom is there. The stepfather had assaulted her and then threatened to kill the little boy."

"Holy shit. Faith could have really been hurt and that kid possibly killed if he got away with nabbing him," Paulie said.

"The police who responded to the assault called it in to us right away and we sent the two officers here. They were across town. Luckily Faith intervened. Anyway, the kid refuses to go with anyone but Faith. She's amazing, and truly loves each of these kids," Caden said and then he saw them coming out of the building. The little boy was holding on to her leg as she walked, carrying her bags. She squeezed her eyes as if in pain.

"Faith," Hendrick said her name and she looked at them. Eyed over their uniforms and Hendrick approached. "We heard what happened over the radio and got here right away."

"It's fine, Hendrick, you didn't need to. We're going to the hospital to be with Peter's mom. Right, kiddo?" she asked Peter and he nodded but looked at Hendrick like he could hurt them both. Peter hugged her leg, making the tight burgundy dress pull down a little and show some more of her deep cleavage.

"We can follow, drive your car so when you're done you have it there," Hendrick suggested.

"Don't worry about it. Caden or another officer will give me a ride back here to get my car."

He was shocked by her dismissal. Something was wrong and as she got into the police cruiser she gave Rocky a very hurt, yet angry expression. They watched her go and Hendrick exhaled.

"She thinks Brianna is mine, I know it, and she probably assumed Hailey and I are an item," Rocky said.

"What?"

"I saw it in her eyes as soon as they locked on to Brianna in my arms and then again as Hailey hugged me hello. Then the guy came at her. She's hurt right now because of this."

"We'll talk to her when she leaves the hospital. We'll explain about Keith," Paulie said but Hendrick was still thinking about Peter, how he was abused and how his stepfather came here to hurt him and possibly kill him. Some bad memories circulated in his head.

* * * *

Faith felt so emotional, and it didn't help that Andrew texted her today just to say hello and to ask how she was, if she got the flowers, and to check on her. She of course ignored his text and deleted it. When she was protecting Peter, and felt like he could get hurt by his stepfather, she went into instant protective mode despite how big the guy was. She was shocked herself that she remembered the techniques Hendrick taught her and it worked. Her back was going to be ugly bruised by morning if not sooner. She was embarrassed that the police had to take pictures to show the damage done to her but glad it was a female officer who took them. Nothing but her back showed and boy, was it a mess. The nurses gave her ice packs to keep on while Peter waited to see his mom and they talked about options with the police and Caden.

Now her mind was on Rocky and the fact that he didn't tell her he had a kid, was once involved with Hailey and that he obviously was still involved in their lives. He was probably like forty, older and sure, shit happens, but as they talked about many things this last week she'd have thought he would have mentioned a kid. It made her wonder what other secrets they had, and whether he still had feelings for Hailey. She was jealous, very, very jealous and meanwhile she hadn't shared everything about herself either or about Andrew and the attack. Not to mention being a virgin, and that was going to come up soon.

How could she tell them? They were obviously way more experienced than she was and there was an ex, probably many and a kid, too? Jesus, what was she doing? Was she looking for a father figure in her life because she really didn't have one? Was she searching for some knight in shining armor that would make all the bad things disappear? She was at her wits' end. She was tired, in a lot of pain and needed that bath and maybe vodka instead of wine tonight.

As she grabbed her things and started to say good-bye to Peter and his mom, who would be released shortly to other family assisting them, one of the nurses came in.

"Faith, there's a really good-looking guy out here asking for you. Says the name is Hendrick."

She nodded. "Thanks."

She said goodnight and then walked out of the room. Hendrick stood there, no longer in his uniform but in jeans and a T-shirt with his bulging muscles and tattoos, and she couldn't help but to feel aroused.

"You look exhausted," he said and reached for her bags.

"You didn't have to come," she whispered, feeling hurt still by seeing Rocky with Brianna and then hugging Hailey. Her insecurities and scars from the past were making her have bad thoughts and thinking these men couldn't be trusted. Her head was pounding and it bordered on becoming a migraine.

"Paulie and Rocky are in the truck. One of them will drive your car back to your place and we'll follow." He went to place his arm around her and she stepped forward and gasped.

"Shit, did you get your back checked out?"

"I iced it. It's ugly and hurts a lot."

"Fuck," he whispered.

She turned toward him as they entered the elevator. She held his gaze and she leaned her head back. "You didn't need to come."

"Yes, we all did because we care about you." She looked away from him and rubbed her temples.

"Headache?"

"Migraine."

"We'll get you home in no time and help you to relax," he said and looked her over. The elevator doors opened and they exited. She was really feeling the exhaustion and everything hurt, never mind the ache in her heart. She felt like she didn't even have the energy to converse with them, to listen to any lies, or any information on Brianna and Hailey. She was spent. She gave her all and then some and she was on empty.

When they headed outside she saw Paulie and Rocky standing by the truck. Paulie went to pull her into his arms but she pressed her hand against his chest.

"Hey, we've been worried about you and about what happened."

"Everything hurts. I have a migraine, too. Just need to get home," she said, squinting her eyes.

"Let's get her into the truck," Rocky said and Paulie lifted her up and placed her onto the seat. She slid along it and right next to Rocky, who was driving. She didn't look at him and sat forward, with her hands against her face and leaned on her elbows.

"Sit back, sweetie," Hendrick said to her.

"Can't. It hurts too much," she said and then moaned.

"Did they look at your back at all?" Rocky asked.

"What do you think?" she snapped at him.

"Damn it, Faith, we need to talk. You're pissed at me and there's no need to be."

"Really? Hmm."

"Hailey is Brianna's mother. We had a brother, Keith, and Brianna is his daughter."

She looked at him, her head hurting so badly she started to feel sick to her stomach. Her vision blurred.

"Brother?"

"Keith died five years ago. He was drunk, crashed his car and was killed. We didn't even know Hailey was pregnant and then she tells us at his funeral. She was a mess and in love with him but the jackass had an addiction to alcohol. I couldn't save him. I had no idea."

"It wasn't your fault, Rocky. We didn't know either," Paulie said to him.

"You guys were still active duty. You were getting ready to settle into civilian life. I was out of the military and should have noticed the changes in him."

"He was a grown man. He's gone and there isn't anything we can do to bring him back. But we can help to make sure our niece and Hailey are okay," Hendrick said.

Now Faith felt like shit. She reached over and placed her hand on Rocky's thigh. "I'm sorry I thought the worst and assumed you were cheating and that Brianna was your daughter. Not that it would have bothered me if she was your daughter, it was the cheating part. Ahh…forget it. It hurts to think, my headache is so bad right now."

Rocky covered her hand with his and then told her to lay her head on his lap and her back wouldn't hit the seat. She did as he stopped the truck by the school parking lot.

"Keys, sweetie?" Hendrick asked.

"Purse, inside right pocket."

She heard the door open and then close then Hendrick's palm on her thigh, caressing it. "We'll take good care of you, Faith," Hendrick said and just as she started to focus on being calm and relaxed, and inhaling their cologne, the truck stopped again. She didn't want to move.

"We're here, at your place," Rocky said to her and caressed her hair.

"I'll stay right here." They both chuckled and then she heard her car and the lights illuminated the side of the truck because the door was opened.

"I'll carry you. Come on. You'll feel better after a nice bath, some relaxing clothes and—"

"Vodka," she said and Hendrick laughed.

She eased up from Rocky's lap and winced. Hendrick pulled her to the edge of the seat and then lifted her up into his arms. She laid her head against his chest and he carried her into her house. Paulie had already opened the door and when they went inside and started turning on lights, she moaned.

"Dark room, painkillers."

"Food, painkillers, hot bath, and bed," Rocky said and that's when she smelled something delicious. She lifted her head and saw the wrapped sandwiches.

"Is that a cheesesteak sandwich from Gordon's?" she asked. Paulie chuckled.

"So Brook was right. She said you eat these as a cheat food," Rocky said and Hendrick placed her down on the stool by the island. Rocky opened her refrigerator and got her a water bottle.

"Ibuprofen?" Rocky asked, looking in cabinets.

"Left cabinet by the sink," she said and Hendrick started to unwrap her sandwich. "Oh, hands. I need to wash them."

"Don't move," Paulie said and then went to the sink and grabbed paper towels, ran them under water, added soap and then brought them to her. She used them to wash her hands and he handed her dry ones.

"You're spoiling me."

"You deserve better. What happened today was upsetting, to say the least," Rocky said firmly as he leaned against the counter, arms crossed. Hendrick moved the two pills toward her that Rocky placed down by her water. She took them, held his gaze and then began to eat. Just a few bites she got past the nausea and then took a few more. She ate half and then drank more water.

"Better?" Paulie asked.

She nodded. "I'll save this for another day," she said. Paulie wrapped it up good and placed it into her refrigerator and then Hendrick lifted her up into his arms.

"What are you doing?"

"Getting you ready for shower, bath, whatever and bed, but first we check out the injuries."

"Hendrick."

"No arguing. We touched on rules last week. We're in charge. Your safety, your well-being is our priority." He set her feet down on the rug and turned her around to face the bed.

She felt the zipper come down on the back of her dress.

"Bath or shower?" Paulie asked, standing by her bathroom door.

"Shower is faster," she said to him.

"Mother fucker," Rocky said and Hendrick's hands stilled, then she felt his lips press against her lower back.

"Jesus, baby, what the fuck did that asshole do?" Paulie asked.

"Slammed me into the metal door. Right against the long push bar. I wasn't letting him get to Peter. No way," she said and she felt the tears in her eyes.

Rocky clenched her chin. "He is lucky that you're his teacher and that you paid attention."

"He's just a child. I found out at the hospital that his stepdad was being abusive for a while. He threatened to hurt Peter's mom and that's why he stayed silent and didn't tell me or anyone else. I saw it in his eyes, Hendrick," she said to him.

"Too many kids aren't lucky enough to get saved. Some survive, the scars and bruises heal, but the pain lasts forever," Hendrick told her. She squinted at him.

"You sound like you understand. You've seen this type of thing with work?"

He was silent and then pressed his lips to her shoulder, slid his palm along her ass.

"We were schooled with a belt to our backs. Learned respect, discipline, and fear at the hands of a man who should have been a protector," he whispered and she was shocked as tears spilled from her eyes, and she turned and hugged him, despite the pain. She tilted up and kissed his neck. He slid her dress off of her and she let it fall.

"You're an angel, Faith. Our angel," Rocky said to her and caressed her hair. Paulie moved close to her, too. He kissed her shoulders and undid her bra.

"I'll start the shower," he said and Hendrick pulled back and helped her get completely undressed.

"Mother fucker. Glad that dick is behind bars. Hope he stays there," Rocky said with his hands on her hips, stroking her hip bones.

Rocky kissed her neck and pressed up against her. "Shower and then we'll tuck you in," he said and his words were filled with promises. Her heart raced and she felt needy, and then a bit guilty. She had made assumptions about them and they were wrong. They hadn't lied to her that she knew of, and she truly believed that they wouldn't. She would have to tell them about never having sex, and maybe she wouldn't have to tell them how bad things actually were with Andrew. They would freak out if they knew he texted this week. She didn't want them thinking she had baggage. Tonight was enough and she knew they worried about her safety and what she did to protect Peter. She didn't want them to know about being a victim. They had experienced true abuse as children and she sustained one beating from a man she thought she loved and nearly gave her body and soul, too. There was no need to tell them. It was too embarrassing to reveal such weakness.

She walked into the bathroom and Paulie watched her step into the shower. She was careful not to wet her hair. She didn't think she had the strength to wash it anyway or to lift her arms.

"You okay?" he asked.

"I'm so tired, but I think the painkillers are kicking in. My head feels numb."

"Well, your bed is waiting for you, along with me and my brothers," Paulie told her.

She washed up best she could, and then rinsed and turned off the water. Paulie was there with a towel to wrap her up in. She laid her head against his chest as he dried her off. "I'm so tired. Emotionally drained."

"I know, sweetie. We're not going anywhere. We'll stay the night," he whispered and her heart really began to pound. Could she let them? Would it be enough to just hold her or would they want more? Would they want to have sex? Did she want to have sex for the first time with three men? Suddenly holding on to her virginity for so many years seemed stupid to her. She didn't have thoughts of this being a mistake with them or suffering a broken heart when they left her, or got angry and struck her. Oh God.

When they entered the bedroom Rocky and Hendrick had their shirts off. She had palpitations. "Oh God, you're gorgeous," she whispered. Their expressions were hard, serious.

"You're the gorgeous one," Paulie told her and laid her on the bed, discarded the towel and knelt one knee between her legs as he loomed over her. She didn't even care about the pain in her back. She felt numb right now and lost in Paulie's dark blue eyes. He trailed a finger along her breast, making the nipple harden. She inhaled.

The bed dipped and Rocky now stood beside Paulie as Hendrick leaned along the mattress next to her. She glanced at him and then back at Rocky and Paulie.

"We aren't going anywhere," Hendrick said to her.

"You'll stay and just hold me tonight?"

"We care about you so much, Faith. Whatever you need, we have your back. You're our woman, and we're your men," Paulie said and leaned down and kissed her lips.

They readjusted their positions on the bed, Rocky behind her, she snuggled up against Paulie's chest, and Hendrick lay across the bottom of the bed.

She closed her eyes and relished in the feel of being in their arms. The protective sensations that eased all those negative thoughts and brought her the peace and safety to drift off into sleep.

* * * *

Faith awoke to the feel of lips against her shoulder. The warm embrace of a blanket of masculinity encased her completely. She felt content, at ease, as she blinked her eyes open and looked at Paulie.

"Good morning, sweetie. How are you feeling?" he asked.

"Good."

"No pain?" Rocky asked. She glanced at him and shook her head. Looking at Paulie's chest, those hard, sexy muscles, she couldn't resist caressing him. He closed his eyes as if her touch was too much to handle. It made her feel confident, capable, and like he felt what she did when he or his brothers touched her.

"We want you, Faith. Want to make you our woman. Want to make love to you, get lost inside of you, protect you and have you as a part of us. Tell us you want that, too. Let us in," Rocky said to her. He knelt one leg on the bed took her hand and brought it to his lips. He kissed her knuckles.

Tears filled her eyes. She absorbed their muscles, their manliness, their hardcore attitudes, the fact that they were soldiers, were capable of hurting her in more ways than just physically and she knew she wouldn't survive if they attacked. A tear fell from her eye. Rocky and Paulie squinted at her.

"I'm scared to."

"Don't be scared of us. Not ever," Paulie told her.

Her heart continued to race. Rocky somehow slid next to her, placed his arm above her head as he lay on his side and he softly kissed her breast. "Don't you know how much you mean to us already?" he whispered and kissed her breast again. Paulie slid his palm up her thigh, opening her up to their view as Hendrick slid his palm along her belly and right to her pussy. Three men were touching her and she never felt so much. Never felt so incredibly perfect. She had to tell them the truth.

She placed her hand over Hendrick's fingers as he slid two digits up into her.

She tilted her head back and moaned.

"Hendrick, wait." She hissed. She felt Rocky's mouth suckle harder on her nipple and breast and Paulie slid his palm to her ass cheek and a finger stroked her asshole back and forth. She was hot, aroused and she wanted more.

"We're going to fill you up with cock, baby, and claim every inch of you ours. Every beautiful fucking inch," Paulie declared and then lifted her thigh higher as he lowered and began to kiss her inner calf while Hendrick thrust fingers faster, deeper. She was coming hard, and feeling so much.

"You want us, right? You want this, to be our woman and for us to be your men?" Rocky asked and she moaned but didn't reply. He tugged on her nipple. Hard.

"Oh."

"Answer him. Tell us you want us to make love to you," Hendrick said.

"Oh God, I don't know. I'm so scared. I...I don't want to get hurt again."

They stopped what they were doing. She felt the loss of Hendrick's thick fingers stroking her cunt and how easily Rocky played her body like an instrument.

She was panting for breath.

"Put him out of your head. Put every lover you've ever had out of your head. With us it's new, it's special and none of the others matter," Rocky said with such vigor and seriousness.

They thought she had multiple lovers. Holy God.

"What the hell is going through that head of yours, woman?" Hendrick asked with a serious expression.

"Some things happened in my life. Things I didn't really go into. Things that had me closing up my heart and making me never truly give fully of myself. Not to any person, definitely not to any man, and with you I want to give it all. It's just such a risk. You're all so big and capable, and soldiers with huge muscles, and Jesus, the experiences you must have under your belt with women is beyond intimidating, and then there's your capabilities as soldiers, as trained men, and I'm scared you could hurt me, lash out at me, maybe strike me in anger and I don't have much to go by here and it's—"

"Whoa, my God, sweetie, you're overthinking it all. These muscles, our capabilities are tools to protect you. We will be so possessive of you because you will belong to us. It's pretty fucking simple. Do you want us to be your men, and do you want to be our woman? No one else for any of us. No other men, no other women," Rocky asked her.

"Don't compare us to other lovers you've had. We're going to rock your world and have you begging for our cocks, just like we'll be begging for this sweet, wet pussy of yours," Paulie said and stroked her pussy lips.

"Oh God, uhm…well, that's the other thing. I, uhm. kind of need to tell you about my experience," she said and Hendrick lifted her arm above her head and suckled her nipple on her right breast.

"Oh!" she exclaimed and Rocky raised her left arm and started suckling on her left breast.

"We don't want to hear about your past fucking lovers. It just pisses me the fuck off," Hendrick said after he released her nipple and held her gaze. "That's not what I—"

Paulie stroked fingers up into her cunt.

"Oh God, let me tell you, please. Oh God." She rocked her hips and then Paulie lowered and started to alternate fingers and his tongue on her cunt. He plunged his tongue into her as his brothers had their wicked way with her breasts and then Paulie's tongue lashed out against her clit before he slid it over her asshole. She lifted up and moaned and came hard.

"So fucking hot and tasty," Paulie said.

"I want a fucking taste. Let me in there," Hendrick said and as she panted and moaned they switched positions and Hendrick was now pulling her to the edge of the bed, her ass and pussy off of it, the cool air collided with the wetness from her cum and then Hendrick stroked fingers into both holes. She screamed out and went to grab at him but Paulie held her arm above her head and then nipped her nipple.

"Get ready, baby, we're going to take you for a ride," Paulie said and then Hendrick pulled his fingers out, stood up and got out of his jeans. His thick, hard cock stood straight up and as he lowered down Rocky gripped her cheek. "Do we need condoms?"

Her mind was in a daze and she thought about the birth control she had and then she couldn't remember if she took it or not. She had to tell them. Did she have to tell them? Maybe it would turn them off? Oh but they were making her feel things she never felt before. They were amazing and so gorgeous. She didn't know if she should tell them or not, but then they might get angry, or think she was nuts being a virgin. She didn't know. She didn't want to start things off with lies. She needed to tell them. Faith went back and forth and tried to concentrate despite their ministrations. Her body was on fire. She knew she was more than ready to have sex, and she was thrilled for it to be with these three men. She took an unsteady breath. *Tell them Faith. Tell them.* They may be pissed if she didn't let them know. She lifted her thighs and held them against Hendrick's sides before he lowered.

"Hendrick, that feels so good. Oh God I need to tell you guys this."

They stared at her and she had their full attention.

"You got my cock so fucking hard, Faith. Stop torturing us, baby. We're a sure thing and then some. We'll put all your past lovers to shame," he said with confidence and an arrogance that came with experience fucking women. It aroused her so damn much she felt her pussy leak more cream.

"There are, were, never any other lovers. None, zilch, got nothing to go by. You'd be it. The three of you would be it," she rambled.

He squinted at her and Paulie and Rocky released her arms and leaned up.

"Are you fucking serious?" Paulie asked her.

"I ruined the moment?" she asked with tears in her eyes and so much emotion in her heart she thought she might pass out.

Hendrick caressed her pussy lips with his thumb as he lowered down.

"You're a virgin? Never had sex with a man before?" he asked her and it sounded like his throat clogged up. He swallowed hard and a tear fell from her eye, her nose clogged up and she shook her head.

"Too scared to. Came close once, and it would have been the biggest mistake of my life."

Rocky rubbed his mouth and chin. "A virgin. God damn, this can't be," he said in shock.

He was going to get up and she grabbed his arm. "Rocky, please don't be mad or freaked out," she said to him. He stared at her body. The three of them did so differently. It was like they looked at her differently. Paulie cupped her breast and held her gaze.

"We don't deserve you," he whispered and he looked emotional and it shocked her. They felt like they didn't deserve her? What?

She shook her head. "I think we all deserve each other. We've all felt pain, betrayal, loss, and somehow something brought us together and it makes sense. I mean, I know I don't have the experiences you do, but this feels so right, so perfect that I want everything with the three of you. I want to give you my virginity. I want you to own a part of me no one else can ever own, could ever hurt or taint in any way. I'm scared, but I know I want all the things you said. To belong to each of you. To be protected and cared for by each of you, and who knows, maybe some day you could love me. I could be more than any of the women you've shared or made love to," she said to them.

"Oh sweetie, you are already in a league of your own. In fact, knowing this, plus how strongly we want you to be ours, I feel like I don't deserve someone so perfect," Rocky said to her. She shook her head.

"We're perfect together. I don't want to think about the past or anyone else, just the three of you, so maybe you should do the same," she said with a confidence she didn't know where it came from.

Hendrick caressed her thighs and held her hips.

"Are you sure, baby?" he asked her. She felt it in her heart and her soul.

"I am a hundred percent sure."

He smiled and then that smile turned to one of mischief as he slid his palm up her belly and then to her throat, stroking her there in such a possessive, controlling manner.

"Let's begin. Faith's first time is going to be very, very memorable."

* * * *

Faith inhaled as both Paulie and Rocky pinched her nipples before Rocky kissed her on the mouth. Hendrick lowered down and began to feast on her. She felt incredibly aroused but it seemed they had more in store for her as they nibbled, sucked and explored her body with hands and mouths. She lay back and watched them. Saw the intensity in their eyes and in their techniques. She focused on their mouths and the way they brought out orgasm after orgasm in her.

Hendrick moved from between her legs and Rocky was there next. He lowered down and licked her pussy so hard and fast she was moaning into Hendrick's mouth. Hendrick cupped her breast and squeezed it then slid his palm down her hip to her thigh and raised it up. Paulie did the same on the other side and she pulled from Hendrick's mouth and cried out.

"Oh God!"

Her lower half was hanging off the bed, her legs wide open. Rocky stepped out of his jeans. He stroked his cock and stepped closer to her, slid the thick, hard muscle back and forth against her clit and then over her ass. She was panting so much. Kept lifting her torso up and down, then moving her head side to side. Paulie and Hendrick kept her arms above her head and they were feasting on her breasts, nibbling along her inner arms and then over her ribs while using their free hands to keep her thighs wide open for Rocky's ministrations.

"You're going to be all ours. After all the crazy shit in our lives, the pain, the fears, the violence and tragedies, you appeared. A damn angel, baby. That's what you are." He lowered down and began to feast on her again, to stroke her pussy and her asshole with fingers and tongue. Then he lifted up.

"Are you ready for us, baby? One after the next."

"Yes. Yes, I want the three of you to take my virginity, to have all of me, please, Rocky," she said and lifted her torso again.

"With pleasure, baby," Paulie told her as he and Hendrick released her thighs and Rocky slid his palms up and down them.

"You relax those muscles and you give me all of you. You let go and you are ours forever, Faith. Forever," he said to her.

"Yes," she whispered and he aligned his cock with her pussy and slowly began to push into her cunt. His face contorted, his eyes squinted and his nostrils flared. "Relax, baby. Let me the fuck in," he said through clenched teeth.

"Come on, sexy. We can't wait to fill you up with cock and fuck you so deeply so hard and fast you'll be crying for mercy and then begging for more," Hendrick said to her and pinched her nipple, making her lose that little bit of fear and cry out a release. Rocky thrust all the way into her, grunting as she gasped.

"Holy fuck. Holy fuck, I felt it. Jesus, baby." He wrapped her up in his arms and his brothers slid back. He kissed her mouth, plunged his tongue into her and began to rock his hips. He pulled from her mouth and inhaled against her neck. He was crushing her and thrusting into her and she loved it. Felt such relief and happiness that tears spilled from her eyes.

"You're mine, baby. Give me more. Let go and be free with me," he said to her and he lifted up and she ran her palms up his chest. He closed his eyes and rocked his hips, still looking tense and she didn't know why.

"Rocky, are you okay?" He shook his head. "What's wrong? How can I fix it?" she asked, feeling like this wasn't good for him.

"No, baby, I can hardly move, you're so tight, so small and holy God, the gift you're giving us. Fuck," he said and cupped her breasts and slowly slid in and out of her pussy.

She wanted him to move faster. She could feel something deep inside of her. "More, Rocky. Please move faster. I think I need it faster," she said to him and then suckled against his shoulder and neck. She ran her hands under his arms and over his sides and he began to lift and thrust a little faster.

"Are you okay?" he asked, out of breath.

"I'm perfect. You're so big and thick and hard. God, I didn't know it would feel like this. It's you. You're so big and we're one now, Rocky."

He lifted up and cupped her cheeks. His eyes were wide and they looked glossy.

"We are one. I feel it. Like nothing else ever, Faith. One," he said and lowered down to kiss her lips and then began to thrust faster and faster as he moaned and she felt the orgasm hit her hard and she cried out and came. He continued to thrust into her, cursing about how tight she was and then he came, shook and squeezed her tight. He rolled to his side and then to his back, taking her with him. She lifted up and he grabbed her face and head and brought her to him to kiss him again. He ravished her mouth and she felt the hands on her hips from behind and then kisses to her skin.

Rocky released his hold on her.

"Hendrick and Paulie need you, too. Need to be one with you."

"I want them, too," she said and looked over her shoulder. Hendrick lifted her up into his arms as Rocky grunted and Hendrick hugged her tight. She wrapped her legs around his waist and kissed him back. When he lowered her to the bed her ass was slightly off and he gripped his cock, aligned it with her pussy and held her gaze.

"The things I plan on doing with you, sexy," he said and started to nudge his way in.

She held his shoulders while keeping his gaze. "Oh God," she said and closed her eyes.

"Look at me," he demanded and she popped her eyes open and locked them onto Hendrick.

"I feel fucking crazy," he said and eased deeper.

"I feel it, too. Take me, Hendrick. Take my virginity, claim me yours please, please never leave me or hurt me, please," she said and he growled as he thrust all the way in and then kissed her tenderly. He ran his hands along her hips and over her breasts then he raised her arms above her head as he thrust into her a little faster. She gasped when he released her lips and her torso and breasts lifted up and she gazed down at his incredible body. Dips of muscles and tattoos along his skin, he was a god, an absolute god.

"You're so hot," she said to him. He thrust.

"Are you sure you can see me without those glasses of yours?" he teased, then clenched his teeth and thrust again and again.

She moaned. "I can see fine. You and your brothers are fantasies," she said, feeding his ego.

"Fuck, baby, you're going to make me come too soon," he complained and then clasped her wrists together above her head and slid his palm down her breast and her belly to her clit. He rubbed it as he stroked into her pussy.

"Oh, Hendrick."

"Feel good?"

"Yes, yes. I want to touch you."

"I want to restrain you. You look incredibly hot, sexy and submissive, plus at our whim. I can do anything to you and you would let me. You'd have no choice."

"I'd leave it up to you, and that's crazy," she replied.

"I like the sound of this," Paulie added and she nibbled her bottom lip, surprised by her brazenness but then realizing that it was because of these three men and how safe and secure they already made her feel. She was doing this. She was making love to three men.

He rocked his hips harder and faster as he slid his thumb back and forth over her clit. Then he lifted up so her legs were over his thighs and against his hips and he maneuvered a finger to her asshole.

"You're nice and wet. We're going to fill you with cock tonight, Faith. Every hole belongs to us," he said and slid a finger in.

"Oh!" she cried out and thrust against his fingers and cock.

"Oh yeah," he said and then thrust into her over and over again until he grunted and came. As he slid his fingers out and then lifted her up to kiss her, Paulie lay on the bed.

"Get over here, woman, and claim me," he said to her. She smiled wide, caressed Hendrick's cheek before she kissed him and he deposited her onto Paulie.

Paulie's eyes widened and he ran a hand up under her neck and head as she slid her pussy right over his cock. "Oh God, you're so big, too. Oh," she said and lifted.

"No, you keep easing down on it. So tight and wet. Our little fucking virgin. Jesus, we're going to hell for this," he said to her and kissed her breast. He suckled the tip and she moaned and groaned, working his cock up into her cunt.

"Show me, Paulie. Teach me," she said to him and he released her breast and gripped her hips. He lifted her up and down.

"Just like that. Take my cock up into your pussy, baby. Slide up and down and work it good and fast. Ride me, get a feel for it. Come on, woman, you're going to be in this position a lot," he said to her.

She sensed Rocky walking to her bathroom and then Hendrick walked out of the room a second. Her focus was on Paulie and the sensations running through her body. She wanted to please him, to be good at this, to satisfy him and his brothers and give them what they wanted and needed to come hard. She thrust back and forth and could feel his dick grow bigger as well as an ache from deep in her womb.

"Oh God, I ache, but yet there's like an itch."

"Scratch it, woman, find your release. Make it about you."

"About us, about you, too. I want to please you, Paulie. Please," she said, sliding her palm from his shoulder to his cheek. He grabbed her wrist and then ran his palm up her arm to her shoulder.

"You are pleasing me. You've made me the happiest man alive. Well, one of three happiest men alive," he teased then gripped her hips and thrust upward.

"Oh." She moaned and he counterthrust again and again and she felt her pussy cream.

"I feel it, oh man, you're so wet."

She gasped when the second set of hands landed on her shoulders.

"Easy, love," Hendrick whispered and kissed her shoulder and then down her spine.

Rocky climbed up onto the bed. "Get her into position," he ordered and she knew what they planned. If she was doing this, a ménage, then she was going all the way.

"Oh God. Oh God," she moaned.

"Relax. We will always put you first, Faith. Always," Hendrick said to her and kissed her neck as he massaged her ass.

"We need to come lower," Rocky said.

Paulie grabbed her hips and scooted down with her on top of him. She felt the cool air against her asshole.

"Keep riding me, Faith," he said to her and she held on to his shoulders and rocked her hips and hoped she looked sexy and like she kind of knew what she was doing or was a fast learner.

"You had that in the truck?" Rocky asked Hendrick.

"I had this since our first fucking date. Then got others. They're in each of your trucks' glove compartments, too." Rocky chuckled.

"Always in Ranger mode," Paulie said.

"What?" she asked and then felt the cool liquid against her asshole. "Hendrick?"

"Easy, baby, just some lube to get this tight virgin ass ready for cock. We're going to claim you fully tonight. No turning back, no fears. We'll own you and you'll own us. We're a family after this."

"A family?" she asked as tears spilled from her eyes.

"Hell yeah," Rocky whispered and kissed her cheek. She looked at him and saw the emotion, the sincerity and she knew this was real and they truly cared about her.

"Do it. I want to be owned by the three of you."

"Yes, ma'am," Hendrick said and slid fingers into her asshole.

"Oh," she moaned. Rocky cupped her cheeks and brought her head lower. She knew what he wanted and she smiled at him. Licked her lips and then pulled his cock into her mouth.

She felt awkward at first as she tried rocking her hips and bobbing her head up and down sucking Rocky's cock, but then Hendrick was stroking her ass with his fingers and her entire body coiled up tight. She moaned and moaned and she felt like she was going to explode, shatter into a million pieces when he pulled his fingers from her ass. She wanted to complain and nearly released Rocky's cock as he moaned but he gripped her hair and head tight.

"Keep sucking, Faith, own my cock, own Paulie's as Hendrick introduces your ass to cock."

"Only our cocks. No one else will own this ass, fuck this ass or slap this ass but us," Hendrick said.

Smack, smack, smack.

She grunted against Rocky's cock as Hendrick replaced his fingers with his dick and thrust into her asshole. Her entire body tingled. The three men moaned and she felt scared, excited, aroused and didn't know what to do and didn't have to.

"Together," Hendrick demanded and the three men began to thrust and stroke into her body and she accepted their dominance and control. She gave in to the sensations and then Rocky roared and came in her mouth. As soon as she finished sucking and slurping him until he pulled away, cursing, then she moaned and panted for breath. Paulie and Hendrick were relentless in their strokes and that coiling sensation doubled, then tripled until finally she cried out her release until her voice went hoarse. That sent Hendrick into rare form as he grunted, cursed and rocked his hips, coming in her asshole.

"Get out, I need more," Paulie demanded and she didn't know what he meant but Hendrick eased out of her ass, slapping it as he did so. She gasped but then Paulie rolled her to her back, lifted her legs higher against his side and he thrust and stroked into her, making the bed creak and moan from his thrusts and sending her body into another set of tiny orgasms.

"Paulie. Oh, Paulie. I can't take it. You feel so hard and so big. Oh God, please. Please." She cried out her release.

"Mine!" he roared and came. He rocked and thrust and growled like some possessed man as he wrapped her up tight and then held her against his chest.

"Never like this, Faith. Never."

* * * *

Rocky watched them sleeping. Faith was between Paulie and Hendrick, lying on her bed and out cold. In the dark room he could barely make out the bruises on her back but he thought about what happened at her job, and how he was there. How she thought Brianna was his daughter. Thinking of that now, he could imagine having babies with Faith. She was so nurturing and motherly. Holy shit, he was falling love in with a Kindergarten teacher who was fifteen years younger than him. Thirteen years younger than Hendrick and eleven and a half years younger than Paulie. Their friends were going to tease the fuck out of them. He snickered to himself, stared at her sexy body, and the fact that no other men but him and his brothers ever got to make love to her and they would be the only ones to ever make love to her. That made him smile and also filled him with fear. He started thinking about her life, about her hanging out with her young single friends and trying not to tell her she couldn't. He thought about being overprotective and ruining this. He was already possessive of her. Now he would worry about her when she wasn't with them. Jesus, how the fuck did his friends do this shit? He had sworn off women for a while, and the whole commitment thing entirely. Not like he ever committed to a woman. There were times he felt like he should take Hailey and her daughter and provide for them in all aspects. Be a replacement lover and dad for his brother Keith. Of course he didn't have those kinds of feelings for Hailey but he would do it so Keith could rest in peace. He ran his hands along his face.

Thank God he hadn't or this wouldn't have happened. Faith wouldn't be their woman. He started to plan things in his head. Spending more time with her, working less, especially in the summer when she was off from work. Or maybe she wasn't. Maybe she did other things. She wasn't lazy or the kind of person to not keep busy. There was so much to learn, to explore. She was timid and shy. Did that mean she wasn't up for adventure like snorkeling, parasailing, skydiving? He was starting to think of more firsts to do with her and then he thought about her virginity. She never had any lover. No other intimacy with another man. Just him, Paulie and Hendrick. Fuck, his brothers were going to be worse than him. They were going to piss her off. He looked at the clock. Four a.m. He needed some sleep. He leaned back onto the recliner, having dragged it in from the living room earlier, and he tried closing his eyes and resting. But then he blinked them open, took in the sight of his brothers holding their woman between them.

I can get used to this very quickly. Very quickly indeed.

Chapter 6

Why aren't you replying to my texts? I'm worried about you, Faith

Faith swallowed hard as she sat at her desk in school while the kids prepared to leave for the day. She thought about Paulie, Hendrick, and Rocky. They spent the entire weekend in bed, making love, talking, and she had opportunity after opportunity to discuss Andrew and what he did but she was trying to keep this relationship perfect. Andrew had no right being part of it, or tainting it in any way. She was getting angry. Then her phone buzzed again. She hesitated looking at it, fearful that it was him. He texted her over the weekend, too, but luckily she plugged her phone in with the power off.

Brook texted. *Dinner, just the ladies tonight at Corianno's. You in or will your men be keeping you in bed all night?*

She blushed and then laughed. Her friends were finding out through the grapevine about her, Paulie, Rocky, and Hendrick.

Let me get back to you in a little bit, she replied and then she texted Rocky because Paulie and Hendrick were working and at the training facility all day. That thought made her think of them in uniform and all those muscles and the way they learned different techniques. In fact, Hendrick seemed to really enjoy putting her into some crazy positions and making her beg for mercy, which ended with him making love to her.

She glanced at her phone and thought about Andrew. She wasn't going to allow him to ruin this for her. She didn't know where he was or what he was doing with his life, but he wasn't part of hers anymore. In fact, Everly called her this morning but she ignored her call. She didn't need her cousin asking questions and especially if she was hanging with Greg again. That life, and their friendship, was all behind her. She had Rocky, Paulie, and Hendrick now, and good friends like Brook, Emma, Casey and the girls. Tonight would be fun to get together with them.

She heard the bell ring and couldn't look at her cell phone. It was dismissal time so she grabbed her things, placed them into the bag under her desk and then had the children line up to leave for the day. She was definitely looking forward to tonight.

* * * *

Conan was at his desk when he got a call from private investigator Marty Fagan. He used to work for the department until he was shot four years ago and couldn't meet the requirements to work the streets like he used to. Police work was in his blood so he started to work for a private agency as an investigator all over the state.

"To what do I owe the pleasure of this call, my friend?" Conan asked Marty.

Marty chuckled. "Well, first of all, how are you, and how is that gorgeous woman of yours? All healed up and back to work?" he asked.

"Brook is doing well, and yes, back to work even though I think she should take a little more time."

"Of course you do, and your brothers, as well, I'm sure. Can't keep a great detective like that out of the job for long."

"No, we can't. How about on your end? Any new babes in your life?"

"I don't like to brag, you know." Conan chuckled.

They bullshitted a little more and then Marty told him the reason for his call.

"So what are you thinking?"

"I'm thinking that the wife of this guy Strayffer could be on to something bigger. As we get this case and start looking into the affairs he's having, including pictures and video, we realize that obviously someone wanted his wife to know about his indiscretions. The dead animal being delivered to her front door? Not sure about that."

"Maybe the one who sent the photos and video is an old lover of his?" Conan said to him.

"We thought about that, too, then did more digging. Came up with a connection to Alonso James. You remember that guy?"

"Oh shit, yeah. He was running that scam with O'Rourke and Manillie through Manillie's construction company. O'Rourke got five years and Manillie got a slap on the wrist and changed his company name."

"Yup, and as we're digging up shit on Strayffer and his company, also construction, we find out from a driver who operates machinery that Strayffer is possibly running illegal gambling games out of various warehouses."

"Nice."

"So I heard about this case you're working on from Detective Fenner in Sussex. He says a guy, Feldman, was found dead, that his body washed up to shore. I got information that says he was at one of these warehouses gambling three nights earlier, and that he was the money carrier for Strayffer."

"You confirmed that information? Because we just got this case a few days ago, and it's documented that he works for a small private electrical company near Mercy."

"His day job, I guess."

"This is good information, Marty. We need to work together on this."

"I'm thinking the same thing, but you know how this private gig works. I'm in it for this wife who is paying me to ensure she gets a shitload of money in the divorce she's filing for. However, her husband's indiscretions just exposed his dirty side work. The feds are coming in on this because of tax evasion and money laundering. The fact that Feldman, his money carrier at the illegal gambling sites, turns up dead and no money to be found is an investigation of its own. In fact, my sources say inquiries are being made."

"Any names?"

"Not yet, but it's only a matter of time. Either Manellie is back to his old tricks again, or someone is seriously out for revenge against this guy Strayffer and is trying to destroy his life. His wife is done with him, Alonso James is pulling out from deals with him, and private companies are backing out of contracts with Strayffer's construction company. He's going under."

"Well, you keep your ears out for me in regards to this case and who may be a suspect in screwing over Strayffer. The same person could have something to do with Feldman's death, never mind stealing what I assume was a shitload of money."

"Six hundred thousand."

Conan whistled.

"Motive indeed."

"My partner and I are getting ready to dig a little deeper. Any incidents at the construction company in the last several years that may be a culprit or reveal a suspect?"

"Just some disgruntled workers here and there, some confusion with payments and checks but nothing too suspicious. Like I said, the feds are involved and I don't think the business will be standing much longer."

"Great, then we better push the search now while we can."

"Thanks, Conan."

"Any time."

* * * *

Marty Fagan ended the call and then his partner Danny knocked on the door.

"Dead body in a hotel in New Orleans. Another associate of Strayffer's."

"New Orleans? Isn't that where we tracked that guy Andrew to?" Marty asked.

"Sure as shit is."

"He still there?"

"No, but we don't know where he is. The coroner is saying the body is a week old. A maid from the hotel found the body. Greg is in Mercy though."

"Shit. Any contact with Strayffer?"

"We're working on trying to track his cell phone. It's been changed again. Last one we got the guys to pick up on was to a private cell number in Mercy."

"I want more information on these two guys. Let's start digging up their pasts, ex-girlfriends, old places they resided and shit. Maybe something will pop up and even a connection to the construction company other than his employment we're missing."

"Got it. We'll catch these guys and prove they killed those men or that Strayffer paid them to do it. It's all about the money, I'm telling you. Marty. The greedy fucks."

"Could very well be. Something will give, soon enough."

* * * *

Andrew was pacing the hotel room. Why wasn't she responding? How could she ignore him? He looked down at his hands. They were shaking. It was something new that started last week in New Orleans. He was getting more and more antsy. This whole operation and idea of Greg's to destroy Strayffer from within was taking too fucking long. The feds were starting to investigate the company and he was going under. That was going to have to be good enough.

He looked at the duffle bag on the bed. It was a lot of money. He could do a lot of things for Faith and him. He could show her the world. Could make her fall in love with him again.

His phone went off. He glanced at it, hoping it was Faith but it was Greg.

He answered the call. "Hello?"

"You need to lay low. I got word that some private investigator is looking for you, which means they are probably looking for me too."

"What do you mean, a private investigator?"

"Just like I said. Stay fucking put. I'll call you in a few days."

"No. I need to see Faith. She isn't responding to my texts."

"Don't text her again. When I say lay low, I mean it, or this will blow up in our faces. I'll drive out at the end of the week and we can split up the money then go our separate ways. Strayffer's company is going under. He's losing his contracts and people are leaving. We did it, man, we got the revenge we were looking for."

He smiled to himself. "I just need Faith and then I'm gone."

"What do you mean? You plan on taking her out of Mercy? She's still teaching."

"She'll get a new teaching job. School is out in a week for the summer. Who cares if she leaves early. I did this for her, for us."

His hands continued to shake and he could sense his mind trying to think of things he didn't like to think about, including recent activities.

"You're taking a chance."

"Come on, you know this is why I did it all."

"Shit, okay, listen, I'll contact Everly, flash a little money, ease things over with her and then make a plan. I think it's better if you don't show your face in town. Stay put and I'll call you. It will all work out."

Andrew dropped the phone on the bed and then clenched his fists. This wasn't going down the way he planned. Faith should be with him right now." He looked at his hands and stretched them out. It was getting worse. He needed to control his anger, the sensations and need to attack. Killing that fucking guy in New Orleans screwed with his head and brought back memories from the war. Son of a bitch, he needed something to calm him down. He walked over to the bag, grabbed the prescription drug bottle and then popped two pills. He then got a drink of water and paced the bedside.

She better not be with any other men. Fuck, he needed her. How was he going to last another week? *Call me, Faith. Text back.*

He reached for the phone again and stared at the text he sent and no reply. He texted again.

"I got plans for us, baby," he said and typed away, stared at the words then pressed *Send*. He walked over to the bed, lay down and stared at the screen until his eyes began to close and his mind shut down. "Reply, Faith. Come on, bitch, reply."

* * * *

Faith was laughing as Emma had them in tears over a recent event at the hotel.

"So this group of totally serious and boring computer geeks decided that they would pull a prank on one of the major leaders of their club. In their defense, the company was supposed to provide one monkey to come walk into the room and go sit up on this guy's lap. However, others thought it would be hysterical to order several monkeys and have them come in at ten minute intervals apart. Needless to say, chaos erupted, monkeys start fighting and one escape artist takes off in the hotel," Emma explained and they all began to laugh and ask questions.

"So what did you guys do? How did you catch the monkeys?" Casey asked.

"Mercy's Finest and Bravest needed to be called. One of the monkeys was on the ledge of a window and we feared he was going to jump," she added.

"This is ludicrous. No way it happened," Afina said aloud.

Emma pulled out her cell phone. "Proof, baby, and over a million hits so far," she said and then turned the phone to show the screen and started playing the video and passing it around.

As they talked some more and were enjoying the dinner and now some dessert, Brook gave Faith's arm a nudge.

"Did you get any more texts from him?" she asked.

Faith looked away and then Brook turned in her seat. "Faith, he texted you again?" she asked. Emma looked over and so did the others.

"I didn't respond, and tomorrow I'm going to get a new number."

"That won't work. Have you told the guys about him? About what really happened?"

"No."

"Why the hell not?" Emma asked.

Faith looked at her friends, who all got quiet.

"Because it was over a year ago and it has no place in my life, in my happiness with Paulie, Hendrick, and Rocky."

"He's texting, and he sent flowers wanting forgiveness," Brook replied and stared at her with that cop look Faith knew well.

"If I ignore him then he will get the message. I also heard from Everly. I know she's seeing Greg and debating about getting back together with him."

"Then you need to stay clear of her," Casey said to her.

"Exactly," Emma added.

"What's going on?" Afina asked and Brook explained and now Afina, Amelia, North, and Kai looked concerned too.

"Okay, we need to stop talking about this and ruining the night. That's exactly why I'm ignoring him and the texts and getting the number changed."

"You can't ignore someone stalking you," North said to her.

"Oh God, he isn't stalking me."

"Technically, texting you constantly, sending flowers is harassment and has the potential to escalate to stalking soon enough," Casey said.

"Why don't you want Paulie, Hendrick, and Rocky to know?" Emma asked her.

"Seriously? Look at them. They will freak out and be even more protective of me. School is almost over, I may not be taking the summer position this summer so that I can have more time to spend with the guys and with all of you. I'm making changes and I'm in control of my life. Andrew is not going to weasel back in and ruin it. I won't allow it."

"And if he shows up and finds out about them, then what?"

Faith shook her head. "I don't know. I guess he'll face reality and move on."

"Wrong," Brook said. "I was there after his last discussion with you and how he took out his anger after losing that job. He has been gone a year and could be even worse than he was before. Perhaps he even planned some kind of reunion with you, and if you respond to the texts or calls then he will show up."

"Brook, I'm changing my number tomorrow. He won't be able to text or call."

"No, instead he'll show up. Then what?"

"Then I'll tell him to leave me alone and to move on."

"And what if you're alone?"

"I won't be."

"I don't like this," North said and then the others agreed.

"You need to tell the guys about him, at least. Then they'll be aware. If you hold it back then you're not in the relationship a hundred percent. There can't be any lies, any secrets either. That's a recipe for disaster in any relationship and definitely one in a ménage with military and law enforcement men," Afina said to her.

Then some guy was walking by and Faith saw Afina's face go flush but she quickly leaned back as if nothing affected her.

"Hey, Afina."

She gave a nod but then turned away as the good-looking guy walked by. He glanced at all of them but his eyes went back to Afina and she didn't even look until she was certain he was gone.

"Who was that?" Emma asked and whistled.

"Yeah, he was hot, and looked important," Casey said.

"You better watch your ass, Afina," Brook told her.

"What?" Afina replied.

"Who is he, Brook, you know?" North asked. Afina stared at Brook and then took a sip of her wine.

"Internal Affairs, and an enemy of her brother Mike."

"Oh boy," Faith whispered.

"Enemy of my Mike? Why?" North asked.

"Probably not a good thing to discuss right now," Afina said.

"Why is that?" North asked.

"Kind of involves a woman. Way before you, North," Afina said and North's face went flush.

"A woman, huh? Something I should know about?"

"Probably not," Afina said. "So back to Faith and this ex. I say, screw it. Change your number, ignore his calls and there's no reason to bring up the past with Paulie, Hendrick, and Rocky. They might think you're trying to make them jealous because you're so much younger than them. I'm telling you, the guys are already saying they're robbing the cradle," Afina teased.

"No, seriously?" Faith asked and the girls laughed.

"They'll get over it," Emma said and then the conversation went around about the guys, and their protectiveness and also how each of the women tried to make sure they didn't come off like they intentionally would make them jealous. It seemed to Faith that all the men were similar in their possessiveness and protectiveness.

Faith felt her phone buzz and she glanced at it. Brook looked over her shoulder.

"Really?" Faith asked, covering it.

Brook held her gaze. "Please be smart about this and at least tell them the truth about Andrew. If something happens, and they never know, they'll be pissed and hurt, kind of like your assumptions about Hailey and them," she added and Faith felt badly.

"Fine. I'll tell them."

"About the texts too."

"Do I have to?"

"Yes."

"Ugh."

* * * *

"Is that a smile I see on your face?" Houston said to Rocky.

He gave him an annoyed expression and then looked all serious and intense as usual. Rocky couldn't help it. The last week they spent every night with Faith, talking about life, about her job as a teacher and their jobs and careers. Tonight would be the only night this week they wouldn't get to see her. It was Friday, all three of them were working late shifts, and Paulie and Hendrick were involved in a case. She had said she needed to talk to them about something but then the week got away from them all and tonight she was going to hang out with her friends again.

Houston gave him a little shove. "I'm just teasing, man. Kind of like you did to me when I was first involved with Emma."

"Nothing's doing, man. How is Emma, anyway? Is she coming by tonight with Eagan and Miller?"

"Supposed to. I know she was talking to Faith about possibly stopping by but Faith is still at work."

"She didn't mention that last night," Rocky said and wondered why. Maybe she wanted to surprise him.

"I think the ladies started texting this morning about it. Afina is coming in with some friends from her new job. Don't worry, I don't think she's been getting any other texts from that ex of hers," Houston said to him.

"What?" Rocky asked. Houston's face went from shock then to anger.

"Son of a bitch." He rubbed his jaw. "Faith told Brook, Emma, and the ladies that she was going to tell you guys about her ex texting and calling. The one who sent the flowers a few weeks back. She didn't tell you?"

"No, she didn't fucking tell us." He pulled out his cell phone.

"Have you seen Faith this week?"

He stared at Houston.

"No. We were all super busy and she needs to get to bed early for school each day. This weekend we're getting together."

"That's probably why she didn't say anything. I shouldn't have assumed she did."

"You know about it but we don't and we're her boyfriends."

"She probably didn't want to tell you over the phone, and Emma said that Faith didn't even want to tell you guys because she doesn't want you to think she's trying to make you jealous or act immature. She really wants the relationship to work for you and her."

"Is she crazy? We wouldn't think that." Houston widened his eyes in challenge. "Okay, so maybe because of the age difference, but she didn't let on that this guy was even a threat or of importance. We knew about the flowers and she blew it off."

"Emma and Brook don't believe it should be taken lightly. I'll leave it at that. But hey, I can understand Faith's fears. She's getting an earful about being a school teacher and how hardcore and older you guys are. I'm sure she planned on explaining this weekend when you were all together."

Just then Emma, Brook, Conan, his brothers and Faith arrived.

"Be calm."

"I am fucking calm."

"Sure you are," Houston said and then greeted everyone.

Faith went right to Rocky. He eyed over her body in the slim-fitting blue tank dress she wore that accentuated her curves and dipped a little low in front. He had a feeling she wore it for him, so his anger went down a notch. He pulled her into his arms and kissed her. She hugged him tight and kissed his neck. "I missed you so much. This week went on forever," she said and he slid a palm over her ass, squeezed and then quickly moved it up her back.

"I know you said there was something you wanted to talk to us about," he whispered to her and she pulled back, looked at him and squinted her eyes, but then she looked at Houston, Emma, Brook and them.

"Let's take a walk outside." He took her hand and led her away from her friends and through the crowds. They walked past the Tiki bar and then toward the side where it was empty. Rocky sat down and pulled her onto his lap on the bench.

"Start talking," he said firmly.

"We don't have to do this now. It really isn't a big deal."

"Faith, remember the rules. When my brothers and I ask a question, we expect answers and the truth."

She held his gaze and he stared at her gorgeous baby blue eyes behind those glasses of hers. She smelled so good and he wanted nothing more than to bring her someplace and thrust his cock into her pussy, ensuring that she was fully his woman.

"You look angry already," she whispered and he could feel her shaking. He squeezed her hip and pulled her closer to his chest. She placed her palm against it.

"A whole fucking week of not sinking my cock in you is unacceptable. Got it." Her eyes widened and she nodded her head.

"I need you, too," she whispered.

"You'll have me when I go home with you tonight. Now explain."

"The guy who sent me the flowers a few weeks ago."

"Your ex?"

"Yes, he texted me several times and called, but I didn't answer or respond," she added quickly and he felt the anger fill his belly. Was this guy a threat to them and their relationship? Was he stalking her?

"I didn't really explain the truth to you about him and what happened between us." He raised one of his eyebrows up at her. "We dated for several months. Things were getting serious, and I was debating about sleeping with him. As you know, I didn't."

He did know it. Felt it himself as he broke the small protective layer and sunk his cock in deep, claiming her with his brothers too. He squeezed her side. She smiled at him.

"What I didn't tell you, Paulie, and Hendrick at the time we discussed him and my fears, my timidness, was that he lost it one night when he was fired from his job, and he took it out on me."

His heart began to race, the anger intensified. "Took it out on you? What do you mean exactly?"

She took a deep breath and he clenched her chin so she would look at him.

"He attacked me, beat me up and I wound up in the hospital."

He started breathing heavily and could feel himself losing control, like he wanted to find the guy and kill him. She clutched his shoulders. "Please calm down. This is why I held out. Why I wouldn't have sex with anyone and why I wouldn't tell you and your brothers about it. Because it would taint the beauty and perfection of what we have and what we shared. I didn't want to ruin this. To make you think I was trying to make you jealous, or was immature in some way."

He cupped her cheeks. "Are you out of your mind? We wouldn't have thought that. Here we are unknowing to what this guy did to you and now he's sending flowers and texting? He's stalking you, Faith. He wants you back. He wants your body."

"No, no, he wants forgiveness."

"Holy fuck, this is why you changed your cell number this week, isn't it?" She worried her bottom lip. "Son of a bitch, Faith, I'm pissed. I can't believe you didn't tell us, that you can sit here and not realize the potential danger you are in with this guy calling, texting and knowing where you fucking live."

"I'm not scared of him anymore."

"What?"

She held his gaze. "I have you, Paulie and Hendrick. What we have together is strong and special and no one can destroy it. I won't let him or anyone else."

"Jesus." He hugged her to him and kissed her neck. He had to stand up to kiss her and hold her close because she wore a dress and she wouldn't be able to straddle his hips. They stood up and he hugged her to him. He caressed her back and her ass and squeezed it.

"Hendrick and Paulie are going to punish you for this. I am too."

"What?" she asked as she pulled back.

"We are your protectors and you should have informed us of this dick and the truth weeks ago when the flowers first came. He's stalking you. Now you pressed charges, right? Did he serve time?" She pulled back.

"Faith?"

"I didn't press charges. He lost his cool because of the job situation which led him to get drunk, to cheat on me and then I broke things off and he didn't know how to handle it. In the past he never showed any aggression toward me at all. I didn't want him to lose his chance of working or getting hired elsewhere. He was already suffering from being declined a new position because he was a soldier and had limited experience."

"You're fucking kidding me? And Brook didn't push you to press charges?" he asked.

"She understood my thinking and yes, she tried to but I wanted it over and behind me. I didn't want to think about him in jail and then living on the streets because I pressed charges. It screwed up my life enough. As you know, I didn't date or even let a man close for more than a year."

"You're way too fucking nice."

"It's over. He'll get that because I'll ignore him."

"It doesn't work that way. I want his name and all the information."

"Brook has it."

"Good, then she'll give it to Hendrick and Paulie to look into. In the meantime I expect to be told if and when he contacts you again."

"New number. I got nothing all week," she said and smiled, but his gut clenched and his concern grew deeper. He needed to talk to his brothers right away.

Chapter 7

It was late when Faith arrived home with Rocky following behind her. She was feeling a little on edge, and a lot aroused at his promises of punishing her for not telling him and his brothers about Andrew attacking her sooner. What she hadn't expected to see was the other truck and then Paulie and Hendrick get out of it. She closed her car door, got out, hit the lock button and ran to them. Hendrick was closer so she wrapped her arms around his waist, inhaled his cologne and he lifted her up into his arms. Her dress pulled and he ran his hand underneath it, exposing her ass to Rocky. Paulie chuckled.

"Get that front door open before the neighbors see what's ours," Hendrick ordered. She kissed his neck and felt his fingers slide along her ass and then right under her panties and into her cunt. She lifted and lowered onto his fingers, needing him inside of her ASAP.

He carried her straight to the bedroom, and lowered her right to the bed, pushing between her legs as he deepened the kiss. Hendrick set her body on fire. She felt so desperate to have him, Paulie and Rocky inside of her, making love to her together.

"Too fucking long," Paulie complained.

Hendrick released her lips, lifted up and started to pull the dress up over her head. Rocky was undressed, knelt onto the bed and reached for her bra.

"Come here." Hendrick took her hand and had her stand up in front of the bed. He pressed her panties down as Rocky removed her bra the rest of the way.

"Turn around," Paulie ordered.

Hendrick tossed off his shirt, undid his pants and removed his clothing. Rocky reached for her glasses, removed them and handed them to Paulie, who put them on the dresser. Her body was as tight as a metal coil.

"Hands on the bed, bend over," Rocky ordered as he assisted her before she could obey his commands. She pressed her hands onto the comforter and parted her thighs when Hendrick used his thicker thigh to spread her.

"Oh," she moaned.

"God damn, she is a sight. I need in," Paulie stated and she felt his palm slide up her back and then under her arm to her breast. He cupped it and she moaned louder.

"First things first," Rocky stated.

Smack.

Smack.

Smack.

Smack.

"Oh Rocky. Rocky!" she cried out and her cream dripped from her cunt. A thick finger slid along her pussy and then to her asshole.

"She fucking likes it," Rocky stated and then she felt the nip to her ass cheek.

"Ouch."

"It's a punishment. You are not to hold secrets, especially one as big as an ex who beat you and put you in the hospital," Rocky stated.

Hendrick rocked his body against her from behind. Paulie slid underneath her.

"I can't take it. The best way to make her see she belongs to us and needs to tell us everything is to make love to her and bind us forever." He gripped her hips and she fell forward, screeched as she grabbed on to his shoulders. "Ride me. Now," he ordered and she did. She slid down over his very thick, hard cock and took him in deeply. She wanted them so badly she ached. Even her mouth watered.

As she rocked forward and then backward, getting a feel for his thick cock, the bed dipped. She looked at Rocky, who held his cock in his hand. She started to lean toward it, craving him, and the need to please him too.

Smack.

Smack.

"Hendrick."

"No more fucking secrets, and if that dick somehow contacts you we expect to know immediately, not through the fucking grapevine." His lubed fingers slid into her asshole and she moaned as Rocky cupped her cheeks. He kissed her mouth and she pushed back against Hendrick's fingers.

"I'm coming in that ass next," Rocky said after he released her lips and then brought her head to his cock. She opened wide and started to suck him down but then Paulie began to thrust faster and Hendrick replaced his fingers with his cock and it was on. They were wild and relentless in their strokes and their claim of her. In and out all three men thrust.

"Fuck!" Hendrick roared and came.

Smack. Smack. "Fuck. Too fucking long. We need you every night. Something has to give, baby," he said against her neck and shoulder as she continued to suck on Rocky's cock.

"Pull off. I want to come in your ass. You need it there," he said as Hendrick pulled out and stood up then she released Rocky's cock and he stepped behind her, gripped her hips and slid right into her ass.

"Yeah. Yeah, baby." He roared and began to stroke into her ass as Paulie thrust upward. He ran his hand up under her hair and brought her lower to kiss her. He was moaning into her mouth when the first orgasm hit her hard. The sloshing sound filled the room and then Rocky roared and came in her ass. She moaned again, and he pulled out. Before she could recover Paulie rolled her to her back and pounded into her cunt. He grabbed her arms and pressed them above her head.

"Who do you belong to?" he demanded to know.

"You. Oh God, you and your brothers." He pulled out of her, lifted her thighs higher and spread them over his thighs. He stroked a finger into her pussy. She tried closing her legs. She felt too much. "Please. Oh God, it's too much." She shook her head side to side.

"Never too much. You're ours. We own this body just like you own ours." He pulled his fingers out and held her gaze as he aligned his cock with her asshole and nudged forward. She lifted up, wanting it, needing his cock in her ass because it was so naughty, so carnal and such a dominant show of possession.

"Fuck yeah," he said, cupped her breasts and began to rock his hips. She saw his gorgeous body, the dips and ridges of his muscles and those different tattoos on him. She licked her lips and moaned. Then felt like she needed more. She didn't know what came over her but as he thrust faster and looked almost ready to come as Rocky and Hendrick watched, she slid her finger to her cunt and pushed right in.

"Mother fucker, that's hot," Rocky chanted.

She paused and moaned.

"No, you keep fingering yourself while I fuck this ass," Paulie ordered and she did. She thrust upward and pushed her fingers into her cunt as he slid his cock in and out of her ass, then he pinched her nipples and she screamed her release.

"There. I'm there, love," Paulie said and thrust again and again and came. He slid out of her ass, pulled her into his arms with just one arm and rolled her to the side so she was up and against his chest.

Smack.

Hendrick spanked her again but she didn't even flinch. Instead she kissed Paulie's neck and chest then lay there trying to catch her breath.

Heaven. She was in heaven and everything was perfect.

* * * *

Hendrick and Paulie's cell phones were going off and they both jumped out of bed. They reached for their phones and then started to get dressed.

Rocky lifted up as Faith went to sit up. He snagged her around the waist and pulled her against his front.

"SWAT business, go back to sleep," he said and snuggled next to her.

"Oh God, is it dangerous?" she asked, but then Hendrick knelt on the bed and kissed her.

"We'll be back, sweetness." Then Paulie kissed her next.

"Keep that pussy wet and ready." He winked and she chuckled and slapped his arm. They headed out and she snuggled back against Rocky. He cupped her breast and got comfortable. He could hear her heart racing.

"They'll be okay, baby. This is what they do and live for. They were soldiers once, and all that training prepares them for a lot of things."

"Not everything, though," she whispered.

He lifted up and pulled her underneath him. He had to lean on his elbows and half over her or he would crush the poor thing.

"You worried about them?" She nodded her head. He stroked her jaw. "You're so sweet, honey. You know they're tough as they come, those two. Been through a lot together and then even apart during their time in the Rangers, just like my time as a Green Beret. We aren't like ordinary men. There's a drive in us, a desire to serve and protect." He stroked her lower lip and pressed his mouth to hers. "Especially those we love," he said to her when he pulled from her lips.

"Love?" she asked and he saw the tears in her eyes.

"If you'll have me as your man, and let me love you. Let us love you."

"I think I love you, too," she whispered.

He aligned his cock with her pussy, and she widened her thighs so he could lift up and press into her.

"You think you love me?"

"I know I love you, and Paulie and Hendrick too."

"You can tell them later. For now, why don't I show you just how much I love you and this sexy little body." He began to thrust into her and she held his gaze and ran her palms up and down his chest. He loved the feel of her, the scent of her shampoo and the feel of her in his arms. He grabbed her ass as he lifted and thrust harder, deeper into her pussy. She tried holding on to him and he knew he was partially crushing her but felt desperate to mark her his woman. In and out he thrust and stroked and she moaned and cried out her release. He followed and she squeezed him tight around his neck and let him lie there with his face against her breast as she held him.

"I would do anything for you, Faith."

"And I would do anything for you, Rocky."

* * * *

It was total chaos when Paulie, Hendrick, and the rest of the SWAT team arrived on scene. Paulie spotted Ranger, Spencer, Zayn Stelling and Conan. Kernan and Kinchley were getting updated as Paulie and Hendrick, along with the other men from SWAT, were getting their gear ready. They listened to the men.

"So the home belongs to some big construction company owner, Leonard Strayffer. He's been under investigation for tax evasion, money laundering, and more recently murder. Someone sent evidence to his wife proving he's been unfaithful and now the guy has lost his shit after the company going under and he's holding his wife hostage," Conan told them.

"Anyone else in the house?" Kinchley asked them.

"No one else that we know of or that the responding police were made aware of," Conan added.

"What do we know about this guy?" Kernan asked.

"Interestingly enough, I've been working with Marty Fagan. You guys remember him from the State Police," Conan said to all of them.

"Of course. He got shot on the job and then couldn't pass requirements to get reinstated to active duty," Paulie said to them.

"Yes, and he's been working as a private investigator and has given a lot of input on this Strayffer guy. I've been working a homicide and somehow this man is connected to that, as well. Seems he's been operating illegal card games and most recently his money people, the ones who collect the funds at the end of the night and then bring it to a secure location, have been getting knocked off."

"Oh shit. Any suspects?"

"We're looking into various things, including some past acquaintances in similar businesses but so far have come up with nothing."

"So how are we approaching this?" Kinchley asked, and just then some federal agents arrived on scene.

"Feds now, too? What the hell is this?" Hendrick asked.

"Marty and Danny, his partner, are with them, perhaps they have something new," Conan said and Paulie watched them approach but then also saw Brook show up on scene. Danny and one of the feds stopped to talk to her. She looked upset. He didn't know why but he got a bad feeling in his gut.

Conan made the introductions. "What do you have?"

"This asshole is going down, and the evidence that was sent to the right people has been verified. Also, got prints and some DNA at the hotel where the last body was discovered. It took us time to confirm who stayed in the hotel after, and in the last several months, and confirm the matching prints were accurate. It's a guy who came up on a potential suspect list. It was like the killer didn't give a shit, and to top it off, he's retired military," Agent Gary Point told them.

"Conan," Brook said his name as she approached with another agent.

"It's Andrew and his buddy Greg." She looked at Paulie and Hendrick. "The guy Faith had dated over a year ago and that assaulted her. It was over him getting fired from Strayffer's company. He screwed him over and the evidence the feds and the private investigators are uncovering leads a trail back to the two of them with a motive of seeking revenge. He threatened to kill Strayffer and said he was coming after him."

"Holy shit. We have to call Rocky. He's with Faith alone at the house," Paulie said.

"We'll get patrol cars over there pronto," Conan added and Paulie and Hendrick were pulling out their cell phones and trying to call.

"Nothing. I got nothing," Hendrick said.

"You guys leave. Go with Brook and get to the house to meet the other officers," Conan told them.

"We've got an APB out on Greg and Andrew," the federal agents said but Paulie and Hendrick ran with Brook to her unmarked police car and headed to Faith's place.

"Son of a bitch, this isn't good," Hendrick said as Faith sped through the neighborhoods trying to get through the morning traffic. All Paulie kept thinking about was how they planned to spend the weekend with her, making love to her.

"She has Rocky with her. She isn't alone so that's a good thing," Hendrick said as the car swerved and skidded through the streets. Brook was an awesome driver and she was really trying to get to Faith's place quickly. He tried calling Faith as Paulie tried calling Rocky.

"Fuck, I got nothing."

* * * *

Faith finished showering and getting dressed while Rocky went out to the kitchen to make some coffee. She put on a pair of capris and a tank top when she thought she heard the doorbell ring. She walked out of the bedroom and paused as she saw her cousin Everly standing there looking at Rocky with a mean expression on her face. "Who are you?" she asked him.

"I'm—"

"My boyfriend, Everly. What are you doing here?" Faith asked, coming closer. She squeezed Rocky's hand and he squinted at her, now in a protective state just by her response.

"I can't believe that you're seeing someone and didn't tell me. This isn't good," Everly said and held a sweater over her arm and walked closer and then toward the island in the kitchen.

"What is that supposed to mean?" Faith asked, releasing Rocky's arm.

"It means Andrew is going to be so hurt. He wants to apologize and work things out with you, Faith."

She could hear a cell phone ringing and then Rocky looked at her and she nodded, indicating for him to answer it, that she was okay talking to her cousin despite her words. It was obvious she was taking Andrew's side.

"Listen, I think you should leave. Rocky and I have plans," Faith said and walked past her to head to the door and to open it, making her get the hint to get out.

It all happened so fast.

"I can't understand you. What about Andrew?" Rocky asked and covered his ear and turned. Everly ran toward him and stuck him with something. Rocky's eyes widened and he went to grab at Everly but he fell to his knees and dropped the cell phone.

"Rocky?" Faith screamed and ran toward him. "What did you do, Everly? Why?" she screamed as she saw the needle on the ground.

"Time to go." Faith turned toward the open door and there was Andrew.

"No, Andrew, I'm not going with you. How could you do this? What did she stick him with? What?"

Andrew pulled out a gun. "I let him live. Would you rather I put a bullet in him instead?" he asked and she screamed as he fired toward Rocky. Faith didn't think twice as she jumped and covered his body. She felt the hit to her side and Everly screamed.

Faith looked into Rocky's eyes. She could see the emotion, the anger, but his body was tight and he wasn't moving. She leaned down next to his lips. "I love you."

"You stupid bitch. Now you're bleeding all over the place. We don't have fucking time for this." He grabbed her by her hair.

Faith placed her hand over her side and cried out. She looked down and could see the blood. He shot her. They got outside and Greg was waiting in some kind of sports car. Everly got into the passenger seat and Andrew pulled her into the back seat. She tried pushing at him but it made her side hurt even more.

"Fuck, there's a lot of blood. Shit," Andrew yelled as Greg sped out of the driveway and down the road.

"How could you do this to me?" she said to him, not knowing what to do now.

He caressed her skin as he pressed a shirt to her side right under her ribs. "The bullet went right through. We'll get this fixed," he said to her as he slid his other palm up her shirt and cupped her breast.

She shoved at his hand. "I hate you," she snarled at him.

"What the fuck happened, Andrew? I hope you didn't kill that fucking cop. We are in enough trouble as is and it's going to take weeks to get into Mexico. Now she's shot? How?" Greg demanded to know.

"She jumped in the way as he shot at the boyfriend. Faith took the shot that would have hit the cop," Everly said and Faith focused on that a minute as she tried to breathe through the shaking, the fear and the pain. She had just told Rocky this morning after they made love that she would do anything for him, and he said he would do anything for her. Rocky was alive. That was what she had to focus on.

"The cop is alive but I should have fucking killed him. You slept with him, didn't you? You gave him what was mine," he said to Faith.

"Whether it was Rocky or someone else, it was never going to be yours. You screwed that up when you beat me, Andrew. I'll never forgive you for that."

"No, no, you are mine. I did all of this for you. For you," he roared and grabbed her by her shirt and lifted her up then slammed her back down. She swung at his face and hit him in the cheekbone. The backhand came at her fast, stunning her as she gasped and then they both paused as they heard the sirens blaring past them. Police. Rocky was okay. He called the cops.

"You won't get away with this. They'll catch you."

"That's what you think."

"Fuck, look at all the fucking cops. Who the hell is her boyfriend? Everly, you said he was a cop. What kind?"

"I don't know, Greg. It's what I heard from Celia when I asked if she had seen Faith and if she knew where she liked to hang out. Celia said she saw her with some big guy who was a cop. Had tattoos on his arm," she said and Faith knew they were talking about Hendrick, not Rocky. Let them think he was a cop, that way they would know the pressure was on. Her men would be safe. That was the bottom line. Faith was a different person than a year ago. Andrew didn't know that.

"What about her wound? Want to bring her to Basile, hide out there for a few hours, switch up vehicles and then head south?" Greg suggested.

"She's going to need stitches."

"He does good work, for extra he'll make it so she won't have a scar."

"Do it. We can't have her bleeding all over the place, and especially not as I'm making love to my woman once and for all." He stroked her cheek and she snapped her teeth at him. She felt her body losing strength, and it seemed like the adrenaline rush was coming to an end as he gripped her hips, remained straddling her body in the back seat and pressed his lips to hers. When he lifted up she saw the evil in Andrew's eyes, the desire to get what he wanted any way he could. He was a monster, and he would win.

* * * *

Hendrick bent down to check Rocky for injuries. There was blood all over him and on the rug.

"Where is he hit? Where?" Paulie asked.

Rocky moaned. "No...not me...Faith." He growled and tried getting up.

"What do you mean?" Hendrick asked.

"Look at this." Brook pointed to a syringe on the rug.

"They drugged you?" Paulie asked as other officers arrived and were looking around trying to figure out what happened.

Caden arrived, along with Ranger and Zayn and a bunch of their other friends. Houston, Eagan, and Emma, too. Rocky roared and rolled onto all fours, trying to shake off the drugs.

"Take it easy, big guy. We don't know what shit they gave you," Paulie said and grabbed on to him to help him.

"Her cousin Everly stuck me. Bitch. She helped Andrew. He was here, shot at me to get Faith to leave with him and…and she saved me. Faith jumped in front of the fucking bullets. Grrrr!" He roared and shook.

"This is her blood?" Zayn asked.

"Fuck, do you know where she was hit? Did they say where they were going?" Hendrick asked.

"Her side, I think, and no, he grabbed her and they hurried out. It wasn't long ago."

"We could hear muffled voices and yelling over the phone," Paulie said to him.

"We got something!" Caden yelled into the house and they looked up at him and another officer who was with him.

"The neighbor was in her garden and saw a black Chevy Charger speed out of Faith's driveway. She also saw a man carrying a woman into the backseat and a woman get into the passenger side."

"Greg must be driving. They're working together on this. Fuck," Hendrick said.

"Get an APB out on that vehicle now. The feds are at the house handling the hostage situation but Conan said it's these men they are after. They killed other men to get money as they sought revenge against this business guy," Paulie told them.

"Yeah, and it's obvious Andrew wants to take Faith with him and probably live off that money he stole," Hendrick said.

"Andrew killed people?" Rocky asked as he sat up and drank from a bottle of water Zayn gave him. Mitch, a paramedic, was hooking up an IV with fluids to help flush the drugs more quickly.

"He's retired military. Marine, I think," Paulie said.

"Okay, that hostage situation is resolved. The feds are heading here," Brook said with her phone to her ear.

"Great, and they're going to try and take over and get Faith killed?" Paulie asked.

Brook covered the receiver. "No, they won't. Agent Point is legit. I've known him for a few years. He just got a call from some higher up. Not sure what it means but someone has some pull and wants this resolved quickly. We have access to whatever we need, and Agent Point said he was told to hold tight and to be ready to move into action. We'll be told where to be and when," Brook said.

"What the fuck is going on?" Rocky asked.

Caden squinted at her. "Brook?"

"I don't know, Caden, but we could use all the help we can get to track these guys down and get to Faith to save her. We don't know how bad this gunshot is. By the looks of all that blood, she needs an ER and fast."

Hendrick looked at Rocky. "She saved my life when I'm supposed to be protecting hers and saving hers."

"That wasn't how it went down though and you can't think about that. Rest, let the IV do its work so you get a clear head," Paulie told him and the room went silent as they waited to find out what exactly the next move was because sitting here just waiting was going to grow old pretty damn fast.

* * * *

"What is going on, April?" Caden asked as he sat in his patrol car so no one would hear him.

"I got feelers out, people doing their thing. Where are you? No one can see or hear you?" she asked him.

"What the fuck do you think? I'm in my car, alone. This is bad."

"I know. I wish I was informed about this guy sooner."

"You've been laying low and recovering so no one would ask questions. How did you make out with the make of the vehicle and the contact with the feds?"

"I have my people on top of things. We'll find that car by use of equipment your local department would never have access, too. We also are using some satellite technology to monitor cell phone usage, which takes a little time but now that I have cell numbers..." He could hear her typing and then she growled.

"I have a wide radius as far as location goes. Five miles, anywhere in that range and I need to pinpoint it."

"That doesn't sound good at all," Caden said.

"It is good because it means they aren't out of the area."

"But if they were and were traveling by car you could use your gadgets to track them by satellite faster?"

"Well, it's a little more complicated than that but...wait, this can help. I'll get this to my sources and through the feed to Agent Gary Point. It will be a map of the area. Look at possible locations these guys could hide a car in or switch vehicles after holding up for a bit. They may think the heat is on too much and want to lay low for several hours until it dies down."

"Or Faith's gunshot wound is so bad that she's dying and they're panicking."

"Let's hope not."

"Okay, baby, thanks for the help."

"Be careful, Caden, and be ready. Whatever comes through to Agent Point, do it and move quickly."

"Got it."

Caden ended the call and got out of his car. He was proud to have April in his life. The shit they went through had been fierce and to learn her true identity and keep it a secret was a burden but it did seem to be a blessing today. Faith and her men would never know who was helping to find her and rescue her, but Caden and his brothers knew and he would be sure to thank her and love her thoroughly when this was all over.

* * * *

Faith felt sick. She couldn't even pull back as Andrew held her in his arms and stroked her body. She just lay there still in his arms, uncertain of her destiny. She was shaking, her heart racing and she wondered if she might die. Tears rolled down her cheeks, and she thought of Rocky, Paulie, and Hendrick, and how much she truly loved them with all her heart. She wanted to see them again. To hold them again. This wasn't fair. Andrew was taking everything she loved, she worked hard for and he was destroying it and forcing what he wanted onto her.

"Don't cry, baby. I'm going to get you fixed up." He pressed the shirt tighter against her side as the car slowed down. "Is Basile ready for her?"

"No, not yet. He is getting things set up in this building but there are people here. It's not his regular setup but he can get the help he needs and an actual surgical room and not need to worry about clean up. He needs a little more time to get paperwork and make it look legit."

"Fuck. She's bleeding so much, and her coloring is bad. She's losing strength."

"Well, you're the one that fucking shot her, not me. We'd be out of here by now," Greg barked at him.

"What is this place?" Everly asked.

"It's a clinic, but also has offices for administration or something. He's on the third floor of the building so we're going to have to probably use the stairs. The less people who see you bring her up the better, so there aren't questions and no one calls the cops," Greg said. He pulled into a parking spot by a set of trees.

"I don't like this. Out in the fucking open," Greg said.

"We have no choice. She needs medical attention."

"I'll bring you to the side entrance and park there. At least it's blocked. Then when you bring her up, Everly and I will work on another vehicle to use. Preferably something inconspicuous and with tinted windows," Greg said.

Faith listened. Maybe there was a way to remain at this medical facility. Like maybe she could act like she was worse off. Her mind was fuzzy now and she felt cold. She shivered.

"Fuck, she's going to go into shock."

She shivered a little harder. He stroked her jaw and cheek. She winced at his touch, it hurt so badly.

"You made me strike you. You brought all this on yourself. If you just fucking cooperated and took my calls, answered my texts, you wouldn't be in this situation."

"I hate you," she whispered and he clenched his teeth but she didn't turn away. "You can see it in my eyes how much I despise you, can't you, Andrew?"

"Okay, he said to take the stairs. We'll find a car."

Andrew slid to the side as Everly got out and opened the side door. She locked gazes with Everly. "It will work out, and we'll be together, be a family in Mexico," Everly told her.

"I'd rather die," Faith whispered and Everly's eyes widened.

"Get the fuck in now."

Andrew carried her in his arms with a duffle bag on her. "Hold that if you can."

"What is it?" she asked.

"Our ticket to getting you the best medical care and quickly, plus a means to a new life as husband and wife."

She gulped as every step he took up the staircase caused pain.

She was scared, and she hated this man for doing this to her. As they got to the third floor he looked out the door and she could hear voices but she was growing weaker.

"Put her here. Nurse, start the IV," she heard a male voice say and then her shirt was cut and she knew she was on an operating table. There were two women there with him in white and they started doing preparing a tray of medical tools, and adding something to a syringe.

"This is pretty bad. I don't know if there's any internal damage. It looks to have gone clean through." She moaned and grunted in pain as he moved her around.

"Give her morphine and I'll stitch this up." The doctor looked at Greg as she felt her body begin to float and then no pain at all.

"A quick job or perfection? It will cost ya, Andrew," she heard the doctor say and then Andrew said something about money.

"Twenty minutes," she heard. Andrew cupped her cheeks.

"You're so beautiful and strong. We'll be done and on our way shortly. Just relax, let the drugs ease your mind and the pain and I'll take care of you, baby," he said and pressed his lips to hers. She didn't even fight him. Then she thought she heard cursing, and gunfire, but she wasn't sure. She forced her eyes open, looked down to where the wound was and there was blood, gauze covered in blood, some stitching but her skin was open. She felt nauseous. "You can't leave. You aren't finished!" Andrew yelled.

"The fuck I can't," the doctor yelled and then Andrew shot a gun, the women screamed and ran. She heard a door slam closed and then things moving around. She was stuck on the table and tears rolled down her cheeks.

"They aren't taking you away from me, Faith. You're mine and we'll die together."

* * * *

"This is personal, and we've been searching for hours and I know the three of you are pissed off and ready to take this asshole out but you have to do it the right way," Kinchley said to Paulie and Hendrick as Rocky stood by them.

Hendrick looked at Kinchley. "We'll keep our heads but the longer he is in there holding her hostage while she is injured then her chances of living lessen. We have to move."

"We're getting intel on the room, and we need to evacuate that building and get the civilians out first then start negotiations," Kinchley told them.

"Let's do it," Kernan said and they suited up and began to help evacuate the four-story building.

"Go get our woman. Bring her back safe and alive," Rocky said to his brothers and their team of men.

"Will do," Hendrick stated and they took off toward the building.

As Hendrick and his men swept the first two floors, they watched the people and saw their fear as they exited. He didn't know what he and the team would find upstairs. If this guy Andrew would lose his mind and decide to kill them both, going out in a blaze of glory. He had seen it before in other hostage situations. He was trying not to think about those outcomes but it was hard, especially as it was their woman who was being held hostage and she was already injured.

As they came to the staircase on one side of the building, other police were on the right side and other staircase. The elevators were blocked so that the stairs were the only escape route. He could hear the helicopters flying above the building, providing air support, and even the radio contact as SWAT and police were stating that there was no sign of Faith or Andrew.

Then they heard about the feds grabbing Greg and Everly.

"We got them. They stole a car and were heading down the highway when police spotted them," Conan told Kinchley and them. Hendrick could hear it all through his mic.

"We got people coming down now from the third floor. Watch your asses, this is the floor we believe they are on because of the surgical rooms," Kernan said in warning.

As they swept each room and directed civilians to leave, they came around the corner and saw a doctor on the floor bleeding.

"Help me. He took the woman and went up the staircase with her," he said to them. They radioed it in and were careful to make sure no one was in the room as they went through.

"Her shirt," Paulie said to him, and Hendrick clenched his teeth.

"We got him, you guys head up and meet Gurrino's team," Ranger said as he and a team of troopers along with federal agents followed them.

"Fuck, there's a lot of blood, and looks like an IV was used on her," one of the guys said as they looked around the operating room.

"Let's move," Paulie commanded and they headed out to the staircase then up another floor. It felt like it was taking forever when they got to the fourth, met the other SWAT team and then heard screaming. As they looked, a group of women were running.

"There's a man with a woman who looks dead. He headed to the roof," the woman told them.

"Let's go." Hendrick and the team took the stairs to the roof as Kinchley radioed in to the helicopter and the team on the ground. Just as they made it to the door they heard the update.

"Got him in our sights. The woman doesn't look capable of standing up. He has her in front of him with his back against a large metal utility box." They heard the information coming in over their ear pieces.

When the gunshots were heard they opened the door slowly.

"He's shooting at the helicopter," they heard.

"I'm going to kill this fucking guy," Hendrick whispered.

"We need to evaluate the situation, make our way onto that rooftop without him seeing us," Kinchley said to the team.

As they opened the door, shots were fired and they had to get back.

"Fuck. We need another way out there."

"The windows on the floor below. We can climb up the sides towards the front. Ask the pilot in the helicopter where the view is hidden from the shooter," Hendrick said.

"Okay, let's move and if the shot is available, take it. He's at the end of the line and we don't know if he'll kill them both," Kinchley said.

Hendrick looked at Paulie and at the others.

"That's our woman. Any of you get the chance before we do to take him out and not get Faith hurt more, then do it," he said and they all nodded and Kinchley did, too. They were in this together.

* * * *

"Faith, you have to stand up."

"Can't. The morphine," she mumbled and he lifted her up, held her close and kissed her lips and her neck. He was sliding his palms along her body and her breast and she couldn't even lift her arm. She cried.

"I never should have left you. I should have taken you away when I had the chance."

"Give up, Andrew. Please, I need a hospital."

"No, I'm not giving up. We'll die here together. That guy you were with will never have you because you're mine. He couldn't protect you. I can," he said and pressed his mouth to hers. She lifted her hand and shoved it against his jaw but she was just too weak. She was fighting against a drug meant to make you feel nothing and sleep off the pain.

"You are completely surrounded. Give up now." The echo of a voice over a speaker system could be heard above them. The sound of a helicopter indicated where it was coming from and then her body jerked as Andrew turned, pointed and fired his gun at the helicopter. The helicopter went back and as she nearly fell to the ground and he lifted her back up. She saw the men in black coming toward them. They were hiding behind some of the larger utility boxes on the roof. SWAT, maybe? Her men Paulie and Hendrick?

She couldn't see much more because she wasn't wearing her glasses. She needed them for distance and so she wasn't sure what to do. She needed to distract Andrew so he wouldn't look that way. Her head was pounding. She was fighting the drugs and her side was still bleeding. The doctor didn't finish the stitches.

"Andrew," she whispered and he held her in front of him, her back to his chest. His lips went to her neck, his one hand held the gun and the other cupped her breast. The duffle bag of money lay a few feet away from them. He wanted to take her away from here. He was willing to die, to kill her if it couldn't happen. She wasn't giving up. She had to fight to live, to survive and have the life she deserved with men that taught her what love was.

"Yeah, baby."

She swallowed hard and forced herself to hold his gaze despite hating this man.

"Did you know at the time how much I loved you?" His hand stopped caressing her breast and he lifted her sideways in his arms.

"What?"

She stared at him and blocked her eyes, trying to focus and speak, but she could tell her words were slurred.

"I…you broke my heart when you beat me."

"Don't. Don't, Faith. I was a different person," he said to her.

"You shot me. How are you different?" she asked him and she slid lower, hoping it might give the police the opportunity they needed to shoot him.

He lowered with her.

"You got in the way. You protected that guy." He gripped her cheeks and she stared at him.

"That's what you do when you love someone. You protect them with your life," she said and his eyes widened and he roared, pulled back and struck her across the face. She fell to the ground and as he came at her multiple shots fired. His body jerked and he fell to the right.

The helicopter was back up above and she heard her name.

"Faith!"

She rolled her head to the side, the blurred blobs of black and then uniforms as they came closer and surrounded her came clearer and clearer.

Some went to Andrew but Paulie and Hendrick were by her side.

"Holy shit, baby. Thank God you're okay," Hendrick said and she could hear yelling. They were calling for a paramedic. The others were down on the ground and she felt Hendrick's hands on her face.

"You're all battered and beaten. We'll get you to a hospital so they can patch you up and make sure that you're okay."

"Rocky? Is he okay?" she asked.

"Of course he's okay, you fucking saved him," Paulie chimed in as she felt bandages being placed against her side and Hendrick was checking the bruising on her jaw and cheeks.

"Paramedics are here," she heard someone say and it sounded like Kinchley.

"Where is she?" She heard Rocky's voice as the paramedics wheeled a gurney toward her and then Rocky was on the ground.

"Thank God you're okay," he said and swallowed hard.

"We need to talk about whose job it is to protect whom," he said to her as he kissed her lips and then pulled back.

"I told you I would do anything for you, Rocky. For the three of you," she whispered, then closed her eyes and they spoke but she didn't hear them. She was just too tired to do anything else. Her men were safe, and Andrew was no longer a problem. Nothing else mattered.

Epilogue

Rocky held Faith in his arms as they stood by the boats and waited for the supplies to be loaded. Miller and his brothers organized a cruise on their yacht for all the friends, and it would be Faith's first outing since getting shot two weeks ago. He covered her hand with his that was up against his chest. His other hand was over her hip, right below where her stitches were, and Hendrick and Paulie were helping to load up coolers. It was a gorgeous summer day, and they were all grateful for obvious reasons.

"Well, let's get going. We want to enjoy a full day on the water and some fun activities, then sunset later on," Miller said to them.

"With cocktails to toast," Emma stated as Rocky helped Faith climb aboard and then everyone else was walking around checking out the boat before they set sail. As they did and left port, Rocky, Hendrick, and Paulie held Faith between them as they looked out at the water, They caressed her hair, kissed her bare shoulders and told her how much they loved her.

"This is so beautiful. Every day is a blessing, guys, you know that, right?" she asked.

"Oh, we know that. Faith, and it's been a blessing since you said yes to being our woman. We love you so much," Paulie told her.

"I love you guys, too."

"How is your stomach feeling now? Better than when we first got up?" Hendrick asked her.

"Much better." She smiled and then Emma approached with one of the crew members carrying mimosas. They started passing them around and Rocky saw Faith decline. He squinted at her.

"I thought you liked those."

"Oh, I love them, but I won't be able to have them for a while," she said as she looked at them and held their gazes.

"Why not?" Hendrick asked.

She looked around them and then Rocky caressed her hip.

"It won't be good for the baby," she whispered.

"Excuse me?" Paulie asked.

"What?" Hendrick asked. She chuckled and then nibbled her bottom lip.

"I'm pretty sure I'm pregnant."

"Oh my God, how do you know? How did you find out?" Rocky asked.

"Well, I kind of lost track of things several weeks ago, and missed my period, and well, it's three weeks late, I've been nauseous in the morning and well, I took a test yesterday."

"Yesterday?" Rocky asked.

"Are you happy or is this a bad thing? We didn't even talk about—"

Rocky was shocked but thrilled beyond belief as he lifted her up into his arms, being careful of her stitches and he kissed her deeply. Then he passed her to Hendrick, who kissed her next and then to Paulie.

"What the hell is going on over here?" Houston asked as their friends gathered closer.

"We're having a baby!" Rocky yelled out and everyone started to congratulate them and give hugs and handshakes. Rocky looked at Paulie and Hendrick and they hugged one another, slapped their backs and smiled.

"One sexy little school teacher done rocked our worlds," Paulie said and she laughed and hugged Paulie around the waist.

"She's in a heap of trouble for keeping this secret though," he said to her and gave her a serious squint.

Faith stepped closer and ran her palms up Rocky's chest. "And you think I didn't do that on purpose," she whispered.

His brothers chuckled as Rocky pulled her into his arms and ran a palm over her ass. He gave it a smack. "Just wait until we get you home, sugar."

He suckled against her neck and she laughed and swatted at his shoulder as his brothers laughed and happiness filled Rocky's heart.

They were finally going to have a family. Faith brought them back together, she healed their hearts, helped them to believe in love, and they would do anything for their woman, and he knew she would do anything for them, as well.

THE END
WWW.DIXIELYNNDWYER.COM

Siren Publishing, Inc.
www.SirenPublishing.com